GUNMAN'S CONTRACT

GUNMAN'S CONTRACT

by

Dave Hooker

Dales Large Print Books
Long Preston, North Yorkshire,
BD23 4ND, England.

British Library Cataloguing in Publication Data.

Hooker, Dave
    Gunman's contract.

    A catalogue record of this book is
    available from the British Library

    ISBN   978-1-84262-488-3 pbk

First published in Great Britain in 1993 by Robert Hale Limited

Copyright © Dave Hooker 1993

Cover illustration © Koenig by arrangement with
Norma Editorial S.A.

Published in Large Print 2007 by arrangement with
Robert Hale Ltd.

Dales Large Print is an imprint of Library Magna Books Ltd.

Printed and bound in Great Britain by
T.J. (International) Ltd., Cornwall, PL28 8RW

To Anthony

ONE

Jack Hoffmann reined his strong, roan mare to a halt on the edge of a stubby hillock, just outside the fast growing frontier town of Indian Wells. Behind him stood the Washakie Ridge, 2000 feet of elm, oak, cedar and sage-brush. The lower slopes, interspersed with scrub grass and wild flowers, rose up behind him to meet rimrock and hill.

Hoffmann was tall, slim, about six feet one, and sat on the horse as if he had grown there. His eyes slitted beneath a low-crowned, black stetson in the bright, dusty light of a waning late summer sun. Tall and dark. Dark man with dark eyes. The sort of eyes that could look right through you. He patted the horse. 'Quiet Jess. Quiet girl.' The animal shook its head gently and snickered, then became as still as its master.

He was no more than a quarter of a mile from the outskirts of the frontier town watching Sheriff Schofield on his early evening rounds. Lights were now spilling out from several buildings on either side of

9

the street and, in particular, from the two saloons from which also drifted faint sounds of tinny, hard-played pianos, banter and song. The tall man prodded Jess's flanks gently and the horse started to pick its way down a track on the hillside, among wild grass and summer flowers. Horse and rider entered town ten minutes later.

At the end of Main, stood an old-wind-pump. It creaked and spurted an intermittent flow of water into a dirty catchment tank beneath. Jess snickered at the smell. Hoffmann dismounted, picked up an iron-bound wooden bucket from a peg on the end, stirred the dust coated surface and filled the bucket. 'OK drink your fill.' His voice was quiet and oddly gentle. The windmill squeaked monotonously above, merging with the everyday noises of people and animals starting to wind down after a long, hard day. When the horse had slaked its thirst Hoffmann mounted and walked the animal slowly down Main, taking in everything that he could. A man like him could never be quite sure when his life might depend on some fine point of local knowledge. He was new to the town.

Schofield came out of the Wells Fargo freight

office and stood quietly. He saw the stranger and followed his slow, easy movement down Main with studied interest. He was fairly sure that this newcomer was a gunman, but couldn't say why. The hard planes of the rider's face were now clearly visible, as he sat comfortably on an army pattern McClellan saddle. Most cavalry regiments had used the McClellan pattern and many of them were now in civilian hands. He wondered if the stranger had some connection with the army? A burlap bag hung from the saddle horn and a gunny sack each side of the cantle. The rider's clothing was dusty, in keeping with a long, hard ride. His fringed buckskin jacket, black pants and close fitting leather chaparejos for protection against the thorns of chaparral and mesquite, had seen better days. In his saddleholster protruded the butt of a Winchester carbine. Normal enough, but Schofield's instinctive reaction was to smell real danger.

Unusually mounted side arms on the man's gunbelt finally convinced him. A Colt Peacemaker in a cut-away holster was tied down on his right thigh. The lawman crossed the street to get a closer look. He saw something very unusual – a shortened scattergun, the barrel no more than twelve inches long on the rider's left. The weapon was hanging from a specially made scabbard fastened to the gunbelt, positioned cross-draw style; the butt reworked into a smooth, polished hand-grip.

In complete contrast to the rest of the range-worn individual, Schofield watched the late sun reflecting on shining leather, steel and brass of his gun rig, as if the stranger considered his weaponry the only thing about himself to warrant attention and pride. A lot of gunfighters roaming around the West, he knew, were considered by many to be nothing more than psychopathic killers. The sheriff eased his hand near to his own revolver and watched the man do the same. It was an almost indiscernible move-ment, the same easy pace of man and horse moving as one.

'Evenin'. I'm Sheriff Schofield: the law around here. We don't want no trouble in this here town, son, and it's my job to see we don't get any!' His words were calm, authoritative, very firm. He knew his job.

The man continued riding and stopped in front of the lawman. He said nothing.

Schofield looked up into a young, hard face and into eyes that bore back at him like black holes. He looked the kind of man a woman would call handsome, then thrill at the atmosphere of suppressed tension surrounding him. A man might put him down as one more cowboy drifting through. But for that rig.

'You hear me, stranger?'

'I do that, Sheriff.' The voice was quiet. Its timbre held strength.

'You fixing to stay around these here parts for long?'

The man shook his head. 'Business for a few days. Where can I get board?'

'Rooming-house down on the left. Turning opposite the Lucky Dollar.'

The two men stood staring at each other for long moments and then Hoffmann touched the rim of his hat and reined the horse off down Main at the same easy pace, to leave Schofield, legs apart and hands on hips, staring after.

He rode along past the freight depot, a hotel with a dim light in its lobby and an old man asleep up on the stoop in a rocking chair, across a narrow side-street, past a builder's yard rich with smells of lumber and tar, past a livery and corral, horses frisking and whinnying; on by a farrier and smith, the latter still working in the bright glow of his hearth, the ring of hammer striking and bouncing off steel. He continued past a barber, assay office, gunsmith, harnessmaker, dry-goods, and an empty shop. All of this Hoffmann saw at one glance as he passed by. He remembered all – clearly.

Lights spilled out from a large saloon on the right. Horses at the hitching-rail, their heads down, long tails switching to and fro. Above, the high false front announced its name in garish lettering. The Lucky Dollar Saloon was in full swing. Opposite was a turning and a few yards down a sign fronted the rooming-house, a white clapboard building, giving the name of the owner as Mrs Stevens.

Hoffmann booked into the cleanly run establishment, rode Jess down to the livery stables and walked back. Less than an hour saw the man fed, bathed and ready for a half-hour out on the porch, before trying the bars and seeking out any information available for the business he had been paid to do.

It was still light when he walked out on to the small verandah and sat down in a wicker chair. It was a beautiful late evening. In that part of the territory dusk lasted for a long while in late summer. He built himself a quirley, struck a red-head on the heel of his

14

boot and lit up. The tobacco tasted as good as the evening smelled; he tipped his black stetson low over his eyes and put a leg up on the wooden verandah rail. As he did so, a grizzled voice broke his new reverie.

'Howdy, pilgrim. Mighty fine evenin'.'

Jack Hoffmann slowly pushed up the brim of his stetson and looked into the worn features of an oldtimer. The man stood on the back of a small buckboard piled high with provisions, just outside the rooming-house. He was as thin as a rattler and had a wiry, grey-white beard, twinkling steel blue eyes that shone out of a battered face like slightly disreputable jewels. He wore a ring-tailed racoon-skin hat, perched squarely on the top of his head, its long furry tail resting on the shoulder of a dark, coarsely woven top coat. 'Yuh a stranger to these parts?'

Hoffmann nodded.

'Guessed yuh were, pilgrim. Name's Sour-dough Joe. Folks mostly call me Sourdough, though – 'cos of my exploits up there in old Alasky.' He looked at Hoffmann for some sign of assent, but got none. 'Been a forty-niner too. Had more gold than's fit for any man.' The oldtimer moved a box of tomatoes. 'Any man who's got enough horse-sense to want to keep livin' that is!' He winked. 'But

15

not being a braggin' sort o' fella, don't talk about it much. Keeps 'iself to 'iself, that's old Sourdough. You fixin' to stay long, pilgrim?'

Hoffmann took a pull on his quirley and shook his head. 'Nope.' He pushed the Stetson further up. 'You know your way around these parts, oldtimer?'

'Born 'n bred, born 'n bred. Whadda yuh wanta know, pilgrim? Old Sourdough's your man ifn yuh do.'

The gunfighter gave him a long, slow, appraising look. The old man's gaze returned solidly, his smile revealing a few remaining teeth and a pair of eyes that twinkled back bright as new buttons.

'I'm lookin' for a stranger in town. Medium-sized sort of man. Nothing unusual about his appearance, 'cept a pinched look to his face as if he hated his own mother. Name of Abb. A mean critta an' some. Got a temper on him too, like a bear with a boil.'

'You know this man, pilgrim?'

'Reckon' I do. He owes folks. And they paid me to find him.'

Hoffmann's words had a chill to them that the old man felt, but he gave no indication of it as he sat down on a pile of boxes on the buckboard. 'Now old Sourdough's not one to offend – you get my meanin' – but you a

16

bounty hunter?'

''Bout the strength of it oldtimer. That bother you?'

'Nope.' Sourdough shook his head. 'Worked for Bat Masterson once, down Texas way.' He shook his head again, slowly. 'Ain't seen your fella though, pilgrim. Not that I recalls. He could have drifted into town at any time. Ifn he ain't been here fer long, I could have missed him. I knows most things that goes on around these here parts, and ifn he's here, I'll git to know about it sooner or later. Yuh can bet your boots on that.'

As the oldtimer gave Jack Hoffman his assurances, Sheriff Schofield eased himself down at a table in the Lucky Dollar Saloon with the four members of Indian Wells Citizens' Committee. It was a regular, three or four nights a week arrangement, partly to discuss town business and partly to escape wives and other more personal matters. Sheriff Dek Schofield was in his early fifties, greying and wore an open, greasy black waistcoat, with a battered star upon it over his checked range-shirt, that revealed a significant beer gut. ''Evenin' boys.'

The four others greeted him cheerfully. They were pretty good friends and, as the

17

evening grew, they usually got friendlier with redeye and beer. Malcolm Chandler was on Schofield's left. He was a big man with long side burns, balding head and a square set to his jaw like a retired prize fighter. He managed the Cattleman's Bank and as far as everyone believed, was the person nearest to being Dek Schofield's confidant. No one ever got to know the sheriff or his affairs that much. Opposite sat Samual Jones, the undertaker and drug-store owner. He'd dose 'em up, so the saying went and if that didn't work, he'd bury 'em. A studious, careful man, the black derby hat and working suit he wore fitted his personality like the narrow, cheaply made coffins supplied in solemnity to his customers. Mike O'Mally sat to his left, an urbane, and kindly individual, provided he wasn't being abused. He ran the dry goods store. The final member was Toni Somerville, the printer and proprietor of the *Indian Wells Recorder*. Still only in his twenties, Tom's red hair and quick mind fitted the image of an ambitious man set to make his mark on a growing business community – if he could.

'Dek, I don't wanta bring up law business, seeing as it's yuh evenin' off an all–' Sam Jones nodded at the bar behind Schofield's back, 'but that fella totin' the hefty gun rig nexta Dan Rooney, looks pretty much like one' them fellas on yourn dodgers in the office.'

The sheriff turned slowly towards the bar. 'Dunno.' He took a long, careful look at the stranger. 'Could be, Sam. If I give you the keys, you wanta trot over to the office and bring back the latest batch o' dodgers here to me?'

'No offence Dek.' The undertaker frowned. 'But I reckon what's in yourn office is yourn affair. Wouldn't look proper folks seeing someone else rootin' in there.'

'Yeah you're right, I s'pose. Hell! I'd just sat down too.' Schofield got up and walked slowly back to the office. He lit an oil lamp, grunted something at a drunk in the cells and started to flick through the dodgers on his desk. One caught his eye, he took it over to the lamp and whistled slowly. 'Looks like we got ourselves a real rootin' tootin' outlaw in the Lucky Dollar tonight, Jed,' he said to the snoring drunk. 'Yessir.' He locked the office door after him and acknowledged some of the respectable townsfolk with a touch of his hat on the way back to Lucky Dollar.

'Is it him?' Malcolm Chandler's square jaw rested on his clenched fist, eyes intent. Other faces of the group, flushed with excitement, looked on with interest.

'Reckon so Mal. I'll get him into the cells first and then have to check back with the county marshal in Cheyenne. Look alike ain't a robber; we gotta be fairly sure before sending out for the circuit judge.' He tossed back his redeye in one snort and got slowly to his feet.

The stranger was leaning on the wide mahogany bar, foot on rail, minding his own business. He stood about five foot eight, had very long, greasy brown hair falling out from under a dirty stetson on to broad shoulders. A large beak nose stuck out from a thin, pinched looking face. He wore a shortened slicker and denim pants, with two rosewood handled Colts mounted at his hips. His once good quality riding boots were scuffed and worn.

The stranger seemed oblivious to Schofield as he approached the bar.

'Your name Abb? Spencer Abb?'

The man took a snort of his whiskey and turned toward the sheriff and smiled, revealing a row of dirty, yellowing teeth. Schofield was close enough to smell bile and the whiskey on his breath.

'Nope. What you want him fer, Sheriff?'

'It's to do with a few bank and stage

robberies, son. Not to mention a shootin' or two, out Green River way. Now I ain't a-saying that it's you who did it and I ain't a-saying it's not.' He unfurled the rolled-up dodger and held it up. 'But this here fella's as close to you as a rattler gets to a snake.' An icy pause set between them.

'I done told yuh, Sheriff, that ain't me.' The man's smile vanished, he turned and spat on the bar floor.

Schofield walked back, dropped the dodger on the table and turned round. 'Sorry, son. Gonna have to put you in the cells overnight until I telegraph the marshal in Cheyenne, tomorrow. I take it you'll come peaceable?'

Suddenly, drinkers moved away from the bar, chairs squeaked on dry floor boards and saloon girls moved towards the staircase.

Fury suddenly showed on the man's face now, and an evil leer spread across his weasely features. 'No. I danged well ain't. No sonofabitch is a-taking me anywheres. Especially an old has-been shit, lik'n you!'

There was perceptible movement of Sheriff Schofield's hand to his revolver, but the stranger was quicker, much quicker. He drew both Colts in a split second and fired. The first slug entered Schofield's chest left of centre and blew blood and gore out of his back. The second drilled a neat hole just above the bridge of his nose and came out behind, taking the rear of his cranium away together with grey brain matter and fluid which cascaded out across the table behind and over a wall. Such was the force the two bullets had upon human flesh, the already dead sheriff was thrown up high on to the table by the impact, before he slid and fell back to the floor and rolled over amongst a clatter of bent-wood saloon chairs.

Jack Hoffmann and Sourdough ran down the side street and into Main. They were joined by at least forty townsfolk from all directions who heard the shots. Near panic spilled out of the Lucky Dollar along with its occupants, as cries went up that Sheriff Schofield had been shot. Saloon girls, who were at best tarts out for a good time and at worst common whores, fell on to the street among town dignitaries, business men, drifters, range men, and card-sharps. The hubbub of voices was as high as the adrenalin. They all gathered in a large semi-circle opposite the saloon, waiting for something to happen.

Indian Wells' only deputy had resigned two months before and no one had been tempted by the ten dollars a month salary to take his place.

Soon the voice of Malcolm Chandler, head of the Citizens' Committee, was heard asking for volunteers with arms experience to join him and take the gunman into custody. There were no takers. Then he mentioned the name of Spencer Abb.

'That's yuh man, pilgrim. That's yuh man!' Sourdough looked up at the tall figure beside him and grinned. ''Course old Sourdough don't mean no offence yuh understand, but are youse a-gonna go in there an' git that varmint or stay here with the womenfolk and us oldtimers?' He paused then added, ''Course I'd go with yuh like a flash ifn' it wern't fur the bullet wound in mah leg.'

Hoffmann looked down at him. 'Ain't seen you limpin' none.'

'Comes and goes pilgrim, comes and goes.'

Jack Hoffmann had changed from his range-gear and was dressed all in black now. The gun rig was burnished, the short scattergun hung on his left hip and the Colt in its cut-away holster, was at his right. The bounty hunter stepped forward, his deep voice rang out calm and clear.

'I'm going in there to take him, Mr Chandler. That is, if yuh have no objections. He's mine alone. I don't want no back up.' He turned to the crowd. 'Yuh all hear me – no back up. Don't want any of yuh good folks gettin' hurt.' Hoffmann looked across to the big, square figure of Malcolm Chandler, standing at the centre of the arc of towns-folk. 'Agreed Mr Chandler?'

'Agreed, Mr Hoffmann.'

The gunfighter paused. 'Yuh know my name?'

'A name like yours travels fast in these parts. And in this town I gets to hear most things that go on, Mr Hoffmann. Someone just told me. Should you walk out afterwards safely, I would like to discuss a business matter with you.'

'And if I don't?'

'A burial at very competitive rates will be afforded you. You have my word as chair-man of the Citizens' Committee.'

Hoffmann nodded. 'Mighty kind. You have a real friendly town here Mr Chandler.' He looked across the street at the saloon. 'Is there a back entrance to the saloon, or any way I can get in undetected?'

Chandler looked at the owner.

'Back door's shut and locked, same for the windows. Sorry, mister.'

Hoffmann nodded. He turned, walked

across the road and up on to the boardwalk at the other side in silence, save only for the gentle ringing of spiked rowels revolving at the end of his spurs. He knew that if his adversary made play as he became visible in the doorway, it would be the moment of greatest danger for him. This was the only way though – and with one big advantage! If a man saw a potential adversary standing openly in a doorway, the only conclusion that could be drawn, was to assume him either very stupid or very good. The latter sometimes played on men's minds and scared them. Enough sometimes to slow reactions into that vital mistake.

The tall gunfighter held his breath. He was near silhouette as he turned slowly against the outspill of light over the batwing doors, and looked inside.

TWO

Inside Lucky Dollar, the killer of Sheriff Schofield stood at the bar drinking redeye, just as he had been before the incident. He looked unconcerned by events, almost as if nothing had really happened worth bothering about. The sheriff's body lay on the floor by the table, heel-flies buzzing around it, hungrily. Hoskins, the fat barkeep, was standing behind the bar and sweating like a pig as he attended to his only customer – sheer terror written into his demeanour beneath haggard features, like a sheep trapped by a ravenous wolf. The swamper had been sweeping the stairwell when the gun fight had taken place. He was elderly and rather simple, earning a living in the town as sweeper and errand boy for most of his life. Such was his terror now at the incident, he had remained all the while standing by the bottom of the stair, back against the wall, his broom clenched in an upright position, held tightly in whitened fists like a soldier on parade. Tables and chairs overturned and disarrayed by the crowd in their haste to get out of the saloon as quickly as possible, remained as left. There appeared to be no one else in the bar room.

All this Jack Hoffmann saw at one glance, taking in each small detail quickly. The bat-wings slid gently past his shoulders, grating on squeaking hinges as he entered. The only sound left in that room was from the doors, flipping to and fro behind him like some grotesque spun penny, teetering in slow motion on the fall. All was suddenly deathly silent.

The gunman looked up. His yellowed smile, a sudden unreal greeting. 'Wal, howdy do stranger.' The man raised his glass. 'Yuh wanna drink?'

The bounty hunter looked for any advantage. The man seemed unaffected by the few snorts of redeye he had taken – judging by a nearly full bottle on the counter.

'Never did like drinking alone.' He indicated to the barkeep. 'Fella here's givin' 'em out free, ain't ya sunbeam!' Hoskins, looking like a frightened rabbit, nodded quickly. Abb's voice rose suddenly to a roar. 'Come on you fat sonofabitch, set a glass up fer my friend here.'

Clearly terrified of the demon in front of

him, the barkeep poured out another shot, his hand shaking terribly. Hoffmann stood where he was, about five paces inside the doorway and spread his legs slightly.

'Don't drink with no killers.'

The gunman paused. His glazed eyes flickered, a semblance of reality seemed to cross his narrow, hate distorted face and he slowly looked at the body of the dead sheriff and then the man confronting him. Tall. Dark eyes. Cold eyes, that were looking right through him. He put down the glass and moved away from the bar. A measure of fear had merged with the hate. But not yet enough to satisfy Hoffmann. If he was going to disarm the man he needed much more than this.

'Your name Spencer Abb?'

Before the last syllable had left Hoffmann's lips, Abb's statue-like form burst into life. He was whiplash quick, drawing both Colts clear of leather before the gunfighter had him fully lined up. Jack Hoffmann was a split second from certain death when, from a crouched position, he fanned the Peace-maker's hammer and blew the fast moving killer from this world and on to his Maker. The force of his slugs spun the gunman round, revealing two bloody red holes in his back, the size of a large man's fist. Spencer Abb dropped over the counter top, knocking the bottle of redeye and glasses across the bar and then, sliding across the gore spattered counter, slowly fell to the floor.

Hoskins stood at his bar, fat, sweating and very white faced. Gunsmoke wreathed the space between them. He stared into the .45 barrel of Hoffmann's revolver and slowly raised his hands.

'Have yourself a drink bartender – you've earned one.' Hoffmann slid the hot revolver back in his holster. 'That was pretty cool work yuh just did. Something ta tell yuh grandchildren about.'

Hoskins suddenly beamed. 'You think so mister?'

Hoffmann nodded and indicated to the swamper. He was still by the stair, stiff as a poker, both hands on the broom and at full attention.

The barkeep looked round. 'Come on Wilf, we'd best get you upstairs for a sit down.' Hoskins lifted the flap of the counter, smiled briefly at the gunfighter and walked across to the stair. His sudden realisation of the old man's state, seemingly taking away all thought of his own very close call with Jehovah.

As the two started on the first steps, Hoffmann heard quiet footfalls on the boardwalk outside. Lightning quick, he spun round, cocked the Peacemaker and brought it into killing position once more. Slowly the square set face of a cautious Malcolm Chandler appeared over the batwings, illuminated by light from the saloon. With him, Hoffmann could make out the outline of two men hefting Winchester carbines.

'OK Mister Chandler. The work's done. Yuh can come in if yuh want to.'

Early next day, the four men of Indian Wells Citizens' Committee sat in the large room above the offices of the town's only newspaper, run and part owned by the red-haired young man, Tom Somerville. With them was Jack Hoffmann.

'We've all had a brief talk Mister Hoffmann and agreed to let you know about some highly confidential information that is best kept to yourself – in fact I will want your word, sir, that what is told to you this day, in confidence, will go no further than these four walls. Do I so have your word?'

Hoffmann leaned back in a tall, winged armchair and nodded. 'I guess you do. Sounds mighty important to warrant all this care, gentlemen. If yuh are going to offer me the position of sheriff, I must decline the offer.'

Chandler looked at the others. 'No Mister Hoffmann, it's a far more important matter than our much loved town. Yessir. I'll come straight to the point. The President of this great United States of America, has sent his own personal secretary and confidant, a man called Silas Smith to Indian Wells for a private meeting with us, the Citizens' Committee and our now late sheriff, Dek Schofield. Mister Smith is due to arrive tomorrow, on the noon-day stage.'

The four men saw the gunman's surprise and nodded with understanding at his bemusement.

'His mission is of vital importance,' continued Chandler, 'because the President's son, Daniel Mackenzie, has been kidnapped in this very county, whilst out on a Western Travel expedition to learn more of the frontier lands, out beyond Fort Laramie. Such information could only benefit us all in towns like this. It would show the soft-shells and other folks back in Washington and the like, what the West is really about, and how we need good people, homesteaders and skilled folks to civilise these darned lands and bring some law and order to little communities like ours. Old Dek had a rep as you must know. He was considered very fast with a six shooter and word got back east that he was the best law officer in the region where Dan Mackenzie had gone missing. Dek Schofield was careful with information that he considered private. We all knew him and there was only so much that you could ever find out. He told us enough though to know that he and Silas Smith had met sometime in the past. We don't know where or when; only that Mister Smith is coming tomorrow to see Dek and help with the search for the President's son. What other information he may bring, we do not know. Dek Schofield was the linchpin in the whole affair and he's now dead and gone. God rest his soul.'

The gunfighter nodded. 'OK. So what do yuh want me for?'

Chandler took a cigar from a gilt box on an oak table in front of him, offered them round and, with no takers, returned the box to the table. He remained standing and lit his cigar. 'It's like this Mister Hoffmann. You've just legally and in full morality, killed the man who killed our Sheriff Schofield – the fastest gun this side of the Sweetwater River. Now that makes you a mighty big fella. If you had a rep before, you've certainly got one now. The old story that every gunslick between here 'n hell will be searching you out, is in my experience, vastly exaggerated. Certainly a few fools and hopefuls may try but the vast majority of men will be very scared of you indeed, and with good reason. That is the real significance of what you achieved yesterday. Would you agree with me, Mister Hoffmann?'

'A man only has reason to fear me, as with most other professional regulators, if he tries to kill me, or the folks I'm protectin'. Let's be frank Mister Chandler. That's my job, killin' people legally, for a fee. It happens that I would never take on an assignment if I didn't think the other fella would be deservin' all he got. But yuh all knows that I kill for money as a living. And yuh all knows now that I'm very good at it. As to your point about fellas wanting to take my rep, yeah, there will be men who'll come. Like yuh say, not half as many as folks give credit to. Mostly the rep scares 'em wild and that makes my job a whole lot easier.

'I'm never discourteous to a fella who's paying me to do a job, Mister Chandler. But do you know what it feels like to be a nothin'? I mean right at the bottom with everyone else's boot on your butt? That's why some men come. Better dead, they figure, than being a nothin'.'

The four committee men were silent for a moment. Malcolm Chandler puffed on the cigar and nodded. 'You make the point well. And you agree with me that, on balance, a professional gunfighter's reputation is of more benefit to him, than say for a lay person, who may be trying to settle some dispute or other?'

Hoffmann nodded agreement.

'That is why we want to offer your services tomorrow to Mister Silas Smith, in place of Sheriff Schofield's! Now I can't say what fee could be charged for successful completion of such a task, you of course understand that, but one thousand dollars may not be too far away from it.'

The gunfighter thought for a moment, flexing his long fingers as if weighing up the physical dangers against the high financial possibilities. 'Well, I'm obliged to yuh, Mister Chandler. But we'll have to see what this Mister Smith has in mind first. The noon-day stage yuh say?'

A bright sun stood at its highest point for

the day in a crystal blue sky. The good townspeople of Indian Wells were busy about their varied business undertakings, when the West-bound stage of the Wells Fargo Line drew up in a cloud of dust and to the sounds of clattering hooves, outside the livery stables. People gathered at the stopping point were waiting expectantly for tired relatives, still as yet tightly packed inside the passenger compartment after the long journey, or for deliveries stowed in the coach's trunk. The time: two minutes before noon. Within the expectant crowd was Malcolm Chandler and his colleagues from the Citizens' Committee. Six superb horses, heavily lathered and now gently whinnying at the smell of fresh water, were calmed by the husky voice of the dust-caked driver as he tied the ribbons to the seat and pulled on the brake. 'We're here, folks. Yuh can all disembark.'

Among the six travellers who climbed down, was a thickset individual in his fifties, wearing a crumpled, good quality, city-style dark suit, no hat and a black eye-patch over his left eye. The man had fairly long hair with silver-grey intrusions among the jet black origins, and a face disfigured by a vivid scar over pock-marked discolorations to the left cheek and lower jaw. The driver called out and the stranger turned, catching first a valise and then a suitcase with deft ease among the jostle of other passengers.

'Mister Silas Smith?'

The newcomer looked back as his name was called and smiled, some of his odd facial appearance momentarily vanishing. 'Yes. Mister Chandler I take it?' He brushed himself down a little, walked forward, put down the suitcase and proffered his hand forward. 'Most pleased to meet you.' The man's voice was gruff, yet full of worldly charm as Chandler took the hand in his and shook it vigorously.

'You must be tired,' he said warmly and introduced the others. 'Come, we'll go up to the suite of rooms above the offices of Mister Somerville here, and you can rest up a while. Good accommodation is booked at our best hotel and a hot meal will be ready in an hour or so, courtesy of the town, sir.'

They walked off down Main among the dust and traffic of the road and entered a side door to the offices of the *Indian Wells Recorder*. Smith had assumed that Sheriff Schofield was about law business somewhere and when the news was broken to him he looked shocked.

'Gee. That's terrible, absolutely terrible. The day before yesterday you say?'

The others nodded. 'Happened completely out of the blue.' Tom Somerville's red hair fell over his eyes, he pushed it back and continued talking breathlessly. 'We were all having a quiet drink and the villain shot him dead right there in front of us. Dek suspected the stranger of being on his wanted list for robbery an' murder. An' when he tried to take him to the cells overnight, so's he could check with the marshal in Cheyenne, the man just up an' out-drew him!'

The news of the sheriff's death appeared to have sunk into the newcomer a little by now and he looked worried. 'Was it a fair fight? I mean, are you saying this hoodlum beat Dek Schofield in a straight draw?'

'Mister Chandler here saw it best, we wuz all a-diving this a-ways and that,' offered the undertaker. Smith looked at the head of the committee.

''Bout the strength of it, Mister Smith,' replied Chandler and shook his head. 'I never saw a quicker draw until about half an hour later.'

'You mean to say there was another gunfight?'

'That's correct, sir.'

38

'Hell's teeth. Is it like this all the time here?'

'No. It gets pretty hot so you might say from time to time, but Dek was always there to keep things in order. God rest him.'

'You got deputies to take Schofield's place?'

'No, sir. None. Couldn't afford to pay them enough. Or more accurately, the sort of man who is willing to put his life on the line on a regular basis, doesn't work for ten dollars a month.'

Silas Smith started to look very worried. They all sat down as Tom Somerville's wife brought coffee in on her best silver tray. She looked very excited at the presence of such an important person in her domain and they introduced her. After cigars were offered round to the men, Malcolm Chandler got to his feet.

'I'd like to make a suggestion to you, sir, if I may, which might put your venture for the President's son back on course.'

Smith looked up, his eyes suddenly brighter. 'Go ahead. I'm only too pleased to hear suggestions any of you might have!'

Chandler spread his legs and grasped the top of his waistcoat with both hands. 'The man who shot Sheriff Schofield's killer is a bounty hunter named Jack Hoffmann. He went into the saloon afterwards, with our agreement, to bring the desperado to fair justice. He tried without gun play, I would say. The gunman tried on Hoffmann what he had tried on our good sheriff and the man shot him to hell. I saw it most clearly, sir. The most amazing gun play I have ever witnessed.'

Smith's demeanour did not seem to change very much, although he nodded and commented on the good work that had been achieved by removing the danger from the town.

'We spoke to Jack Hoffmann yesterday, in these very rooms as it happens. And should you so wish, he is willing to offer his not unimportant services in the venture you are undertaking to find Mister Mackenzie's son.'

A deep pause fell across the room as Malcolm Chandler sat down. The others looked at President Mackenzie's personal confidant in silence. The man was still clearly shocked by events, but fighting to regain himself. 'Is this man available to see me now?'

Chandler nodded. 'He certainly is, sir. Shall I arrange for him to be brought up here?'

'Please do, Mister Chandler.'

Chandler nodded to Mike O'Mally. 'Would you mind Mike?'

O'Mally got to his feet, smiled generously and returned in a few minutes with Jack Hoffmann. The gunfighter's appearance suddenly altered the atmosphere in the room completely. His presence, whether by implication of past deeds, his brooding stature, or some other reason unknown to them, contained an aura that was almost tangible.

Jack Hoffmann stood straight and lean. He was dressed in the same black garb they had seen when he killed Spencer Abb. The gun rig hung from his hips, burnished with the glow of leather, steel and brass that the group had witnessed before, somehow reflecting the deathly pride his skills had won over the years. Tall and dark. Hypnotic, hard eyes. Staring. The sort that could look right through a man.

Silas Smith was looking right into those eyes now and he held the gaze with uneasy equilibrium. 'Nice to meet you, Mister Hoffmann. I've heard a lot about you.'

Hoffmann nodded. 'I believe you would like to discuss a business matter, Mister Smith?'

Smith nodded and indicated for him to sit.

41

'It seems that you killed Sheriff Schofield's murderer in a fair and legal fight. That so?'

The bounty hunter nodded agreement.

'OK. The President pays me my salary because, by and large, I get the results he requires – just as you have. Frankly, Mister Hoffmann, if he knew the details of how I sometimes sail close to the wind to get those results for him, he would be a little surprised, if you get my meaning. I don't think he always appreciates what is done. But then the President has far higher matters on his mind than to worry about such things. I am paid to get results. It is as simple as that. Poor Sheriff Schofield's murder is a grievous sin to me and puts my plans into confusion. These good people tell me that you may be willing to help track down the culprits who have kidnapped his son, Daniel?'

Hoffmann nodded slowly. 'Mebbe, Mister Smith. If we discuss the situation in depth and I feel that my gun can help in the matter, I will undertake the commission for yuh. If not, we must leave it where it lies. What can yuh tell me about the affair?'

A slight, almost imperceptible tic appeared on the easterner's cheek, just below the vivid scar tissue and he repositioned himself in the large, winged armchair. A sudden smile lightened the man's face, reducing the odd appearance from the unfortunate disfigurement. 'I believe in looking on the positive side gentlemen.' He nodded and indicated to his cheek. 'Got this little beauty at Bull Run in '62, down at the Rappahannock River in Virginia. I was extremely fortunate to have my life saved by none other than Major General T.J. "Stonewall" Jackson himself. Through that fortunate encounter, I rose from humble beginnings to the position I hold now. That experience taught me to always look for a way of betterment, be that for yourself, or for a situation you find yourself in. Now the situation we find ourselves in here is pretty bleak, I don't mind admitting. Do any of you people know of a small mining town around these parts called Oaksville?'

The others nodded assent including Hoffmann. 'Yeah. I know the spot. Almost dead now, so I hear, since the gold ran out.'

'Well gentlemen, that is the last place Daniel Mackenzie was heard of, so I'm told. And that, unfortunately, is all we have to go on in this matter. I was hoping your sheriff could have enlightened me more.'

Sam Jones joined the conversation. 'There's

a no-account gunslick who's been based up that way with a gang o' scoundrels fer a few years now. Name o' Joshua Soames. It's pretty common knowledge. Bad robber an' killer so's I hear, Mister Hoffmann. If Daniel Mackenzie wuz held up there, could be Soames knows somethin' – an' the wicked ol' devil might even be mixed up in the affair!'

Hoffmann looked across to Silas Smith for his reaction and was surprised to see a split-second flush of anger in the man's ruddy features. The burning look vanished as quickly as it came and was replaced by the smooth, relaxed smile of the city diplomat. The change was so incredible that the gunfighter wondered if he had misjudged.

'Don't know anything about your bad man, mister, but I feel Mister Hoffmann ought to keep a wider perspective in his search.'

A gloomy silence settled on the committee members seated in the room.

Smith smiled again. 'Don't let's be down-hearted, gentlemen. I will find a way to solve the problem in due course. There are many folks I know and I can talk with many influential people. Something will come up no doubt. I take it this is a bit outside your normal area of work Mister Hoffmann? I'll fully understand if it is, and not hold you to the problem. If however you do decide to take on the commission, I'll want you to go to Oaksville immediately!'

The gunfighter looked back at Silas Smith and the man felt those dark eyes upon him again, like orbs of death. 'I normally only ask for payment on work completed, Mister Smith. However, in this case, I will need fifteen dollars a month for supplies and vittles, on top of my fee, until successful completion of the contract.'

The easterner looked surprised. 'And what would that fee be?'

'One thousand, two hundred dollars – cash!'

Smith was a quick thinker. 'One thousand dollars exactly, Mister Hoffmann,' he countered, 'and not a cent more – on successful completion only. Which means the safe return of Daniel Mackenzie to me, a relative or someone in suitable authority. OK?'

'And how would I get my monthly payment?'

'I'll arrange for Mister Chandler here, to pay you via a bank draft. That OK with you Mister Chandler?'

The Chairman of the Citizens' Committee nodded agreement.

'Well now, how does that sound to you

Mister Hoffman?'

Hoffmann's dark eyes fell on the easterner once more. 'I guess yuh got yourself a deal.' He stood up, his six-foot-one-frame towering over the man. 'Pleased to do business with yuh, Mister Smith, make a start in the morning.' Smith nodded and they shook hands. Jack Hoffmann turned and acknowledged the others. 'Gentlemen.' He left the room with the same easy, animal-like movements that the townspeople had witnessed the night before – belying his deadly speed in combat.

THREE

Two buckskin-clad prospectors clumped up on to the stoop of the assay office with leather bags over their shoulders, and entered the doorway with hope shining from their eyes. One looked out as Hoffmann passed, checked the street and bid him a loud, 'Howdy-do!' The time was five minutes past nine in the morning. Hoffmann was leaving fairly late because he knew the journey to Oaksville could be completed in two and a half days of hard riding and he figured three would lose nothing and give him and Jess a good start to what might eventually be a long haul.

The tall gunfighter nodded. 'Howdy.'

'Looks like it's gonna be another nice day.'

'Sure does.'

The assay door was shut with a bang and Hoffmann guessed at the despair or joy that was about to follow a few minutes later, when their bags of dust and pieces of ore proved either to be nothing more than pyrites, or much sweated for, gold.

He entered the gunsmith's shop opposite, picked up some shells for his Winchester and the Colts, and bought provisions in the store next door. Hefting the filled gunny sack to his shoulder, the gunfighter strode down Main. He was dressed in his range-gear now; a fringed buckskin jacket, black pants with close-fitting leather chaps flapping gently against his legs as he walked. The sun was beginning to climb into another clear blue sky and he squinted out from under the brim of a low-crowned black Stetson at townsfolk, who pointed him out to friends, or whispered words to awe-filled children. The bounty hunter touched the brim of his hat here and there, to acknowledge respectful tidings of the day from a few folks as they passed by. He strode on past the blacksmith, farrier, large lumber-penned corral, and then turned into the livery stables.

'Good morning to you, sir. Mighty fine day again!'

The hostler, a short, stocky man with a well-trimmed beard and a manner that showed his pleasure at giving good service, smiled and indicated the stall where Jess was waiting.

Hoffmann went into the enclosure which smelled of good clean straw and the horse snickered a welcome. She had been curried and looked better for it, together with over two days of rest. He began dressing the animal with rawhide halter, his saddle and other equipment taken from a lumber beam to the side and from an oaken platform, built for the purpose in the corner and completed by strapping the saddleholster in place.

'Mighty fine saddle yer got there Mister Hoffmann.' The hostler smiled, as he leaned against the doorway. 'Mighty fine. Musta ridd'n hundreds o' miles on one jest like yours, when I wuz a cavalryman.'

Hoffmann nodded and tightened the cinches. He paid the hostler and led Jess from the stall. The horse came out of the livery, its coat gleaming, ears pricked and alert. Taking one more look back down Main, the gunfighter swung up into leather, and headed out of Indian Wells on what could prove to be the most difficult contract he had ever undertaken.

After following the trail for over a day, the land started to rise on a steady climb; the gunfighter stopped at a ridge marking the beginnings of vast, untouched forested lands, that were still virgin free of man and his best endeavours. Giant ferns and wild vines still grew up there, amongst the higher reaches. He turned the horse and, sitting completely still, looked back and surveyed the scene. Ahead, beyond the far distant town, a sea of faint waving grasses fanned out to become part of the great Wyoming plain which, seen from here, ebbed into ruptured skylines and castles of white cloud.

He patted Jess. 'Come on girl.' Then gently turned the horse back up the trail. There was a stillness there, not from the wind, which was now soughing the trees in easy pleasure, but from the spirit of the place. The range-hardened man could almost smell life's essence up there and he smiled, enjoying the emptiness and freedom.

They rode solidly for three more hours among the stands of aspen, thickets of oak and changing scenes of pine, elm and cedar wood, before he broke for camp at just after noon. A pot of fresh coffee was soon bubbling on the camp-fire and a plate of beef jerky and hot beans tasted good. He took out an oilskin pouch containing cigarette papers and his favourite brand of Bull Durham tobacco and twisted up a quirley. Jess whickered gently, as if aware of the sun's progress. Hoffmann climbed to his feet, tossed the remains of the coffee on the fire, stamped it out and packed his few things. He climbed up into the saddle, reined the horse back on to the trail and headed over the top of the hill.

From here, a wonderful view spread before them. For almost as far as the eye could see lay a mixture of forest and open rolling lands filled with grass and wild flowers. Across the hillside, juniper and piñon were mingled with aspen, buttercup and corn-flowers, to lay a great moving sea of green and yellow over the slopes. The spoor of bear, mountain sheep and deer were to be seen among the trees, and after the coolness of the highlands, the air was warmer here, yet still fresh and clean. Through the branches of spruce trees he spotted a deer browsing and eating shrubs in a thicket lower down and was tempted to take a shot at it with the Winchester. He decided it would be a waste of good meat and moved on.

The trail wound its way down the hillside. Evening was not too far away now and Hoffmann decided to find a good place to make camp. They followed a natural path through thorn bushes which led to a large, natural meadow. Hoffmann walked the horse across, through luscious pastureland dotted with bighorn sheep and some beeves that had escaped their herded fate by man. As Jess walked, knocking the heads off the taller plants, a myriad of moths and butterflies lifted into the air, becoming a fluttering cloud of colour at her flanks. Larks also rose into flight and flitted away in zig-zag, singing out at the approach of the horse's hooves.

The level field eased slowly to a fairly steep descent at the far side, with a thicket of pine and conifer trees on the right. At the bottom, a minor river bent its way and watered a green valley. Willows, cottonwoods and pale osiers could be seen clothing the banks of the river and the gunfighter was about to head the horse down, still enjoying the solitude and expectation of a camp-fire meal, when something caught his eye.

A glint of light flashed for a moment high up on the rimrock to the right. The thicket led to the foot of the rocky bluff and Hoffmann's highly-honed sense of self-preservation told him danger was near.

He moved from sight and entered the trees, tied the horse's reins to a branch and took the Winchester from the saddleholster. Quickly now his body adjusted from easy pleasure to the high flow of adrenalin that always preceded danger. It was suddenly dark and damp in among the evergreen trees. Fir cones and pine needles softened each footfall so well that, together with the dense covering of trees, he could run in near perfect safety for a long distance without fear of detection. After a while he saw the evergreens thinning and the steep rise of the rocky bluff ahead. The gunfighter skirted around the bottom of the cliff, keeping just inside the perimeter of trees and, when at a point that he took to be somewhere behind the origin of the sun-glint, he started out of the thicket and began to climb.

Here it was not too steep for a reasonably safe ascent. However, the mainly scree slopes of an escarpment caused him some difficulty. Apart from the noise of loose stones, there was the potential of falling because of the unstable surface and, though unlikely to sustain serious injury, he could be extremely prone to a rifleman with the advantage of height, directly above him. Jack Hoffmann took the detritus slope carefully and well, working from outcrop to outcrop of solid rock; winning slow but definite height advantage with every minute that passed.

Soon he rose above the most prone part of the climb and started to work from cover to cover, afforded by boulders, scraggy trees and bushes which seemed to be holding on to the inhospitable cliff-face as grimly as he was.

At last the gunfighter reached the top and, pulling himself close to a large rock for cover, he untied the bandanna from around his neck and wiped sweat from his brow. There in front, no more than forty yards ahead, sat a youngster whom he would put at no more than twenty years of age. The man looked like any cow-hand to be found on the cattle-ranges in the territory; denim pants, faded shirt, scuffed boots, a well-worn brown Stetson – but the Winchester cradled in his lap looked just about as unfriendly as you could get! Hoffmann decided that it was very important to find out exactly why the stranger was waiting there, presumably to shoot him! It was a trade-off between vital knowledge and the cold realities of survival.

'Move one muscle and I'll blow yuh god-damn head off!'

The man jerked for a moment, shocked by the surprise of being completely out-manoeuvred, and slowly raised his hands. Anyone mean enough to bushwhack was likely to be as slippery as a rattler and just as quick. Hoffmann's reactions were on hair-trigger settings.

'Put the rifle down to one side, stand up real slow and turn around.'

The man did as he was told. Little more than a fresh-faced kid, he had all the makings of a devious malcontent written into a thin, angular face, built around large, grey eyes that were burning out at him furiously, full of bitter anger at being caught.

'What yuh doing here?'

No reply came, only arrogance and anger.

'Tell yuh once more.' The gunfighter levered a round into his Winchester, pausing for a moment. He watched the anger growing into hatred before him and squeezed the trigger slowly. The carbine, held almost casually at his hip, suddenly boomed out, shattering the silence. The slug howled off the rocky ground no more than six inches from the man's foot.

'What yuh doing here?'

The man's face broke into a sneer. 'Say, you always go jumpin' out on law-abiding folks who's jest mindin' their own business?'

The Winchester boomed again. Hoffmann levered another shell into the chamber and he fired. Then another and another. Dust and smoke filled the space between them and the stranger moved back, dangerously near to the edge of a sheer drop of some 250 feet.

'OK, OK you bastard.' The face was now a confused mixture of fear and anger. 'Wadda you want?'

'I'll say it again, son, what are yuh doing here?'

He looked flustered and mastered himself quickly. 'Your name Hoffmann?'

The gunfighter held the younger man's gaze like a cougar before a coyote. Dark man. Dark eyes, glowing now like pools of death. 'And if it is?'

Terror suddenly held the kid. 'I wuz told to watch out fer a mean sonofabitch, bounty hunter. A man totin' a belt-mounted short scattergun an' riding a chestnut mixed with white and grey.' His eyes suddenly flicked across to where Hoffmann's horse was last visible before being tied in the pine thicket, and then back to the scattergun hanging at the gunfighter's waist.

'Who told yuh to do that?' asked Hoffmann, his voice giving no quarter.

The stranger shook his head slowly as if in disbelief. 'No. He'll kill me. He'll kill me fer sure.'

'If he don't, yuh can be sure as hell I will.' Hoffmann levered a further round into the carbine and raised it to his shoulder. The youngster could see the gun aimed directly at him, but only as a secondary fact. It was those eyes staring out from under the man's black stetson that filled him with unmitigated terror. 'Soames, Josh Soames – in Oaksville!' The words came out at little more than a whisper.

Soames! He had heard that name before from Sam Jones, at the meeting with Silas Smith and the committee back in Indian Wells. Suddenly, Hoffmann realised that his quarry was now close to a bloody death through his own panic.

'Move away from that drop slowly, son. You're almost on the edge. Walk towards me careful like.'

The kid seemed to pull himself back to reality for a moment and then he looked down. The shock caused him to waver and one foot started to slide on the scree. Hoffmann dropped his Winchester, ran a few steps forward and made a grab at the man before he vanished over the edge. An agonising scream rent the air as the kid fell. Hoffmann had barely stopped himself from going over and he looked down the full drop of the precipice, watching the cartwheeling form turn and cry out in terror. Then an awful silence when the youngster's head hit a rocky outcrop near the bottom. The body rolled and danced across the detritus rock floor like a rag doll and stopped face up, leaving a witness of blood and gore streaked across the wings of craggy escarpment. The gunfighter pushed himself back from the edge slowly and climbed to his feet.

Twenty minutes saw him back in the thicket and patting Jess. 'Good girl, Jess. Good girl.' He led the mare out of the dank closeness of the conifer and pines and mounted up. Looking upwards, Hoffmann could see there was just enough daylight left to make camp down by the river and have a good meal before bedding down. He felt suddenly very tired. The kid was dead. Nothing could be done. One lived, the other didn't. The dead man would have most surely been him, if Hickok's teaching, and that of others, had not become ingrained as part of his very existence. The others. Hoffmann's thoughts wandered back to the hard men who had taught him his craft. He mounted Jess and started upon the descent towards the river bank. 'Always sleep nights, Jack. It's the best rule to check yourself all the way home!' That's what they had said around the camp-fire and he remembered.

The full moon had risen yellow and bright when Jack Hoffmann settled down under a willow tree, his head against the saddle, and watched the camp-fire embers dying quietly. Within two minutes he was in a deep, sound sleep.

Willow, cottonwood and osiers dug their roots into the sweet, wet soil around a deep pool where the gunfighter had made camp. He rose just after dawn from effortless slumbers and stripped off. The air was crisp and cool. The sun, just over the horizon, flickered through the big old willow and rippled warmth across his body as he walked naked up to the pool's edge. He looked a lot younger than his twenty-eight years. Hard and worldly, in a strange contradiction of life: as if too much living was yet to furnish unpaid dues upon him. The man's broad shoulders and large chest tapered down to lean hips and long, powerful legs, that were in balanced proportion to a height of six feet one. He pushed back a swathe of jet black hair and stretched arms that had the hard muscle from many years of physical labour worked into them. A blue and white mallard clucked warnings from reeds on the far side of the pool as Hoffmann dived into the crystal clear water. He surfaced and swam around lazily for some minutes before returning to the bank, where he dried, dressed quickly and had the camp-fire soon rekindled, with twigs and bark of gnarled mesquite.

Hoffmann broke open a pack from one of the two gunny sacks that his horse had carried and took out cooking utensils. Soon a pan was steaming over the fire and he added some Arbuckle to the boiling water. Then eggs and bacon into a frying pan. Breakfast, washed down with lashings of the steaming hot coffee, set him up for the day and all that must be ahead. It was a good meal, the best he had enjoyed for a long while. The solitary openness of the wild was the best companion the bounty hunter knew, and the only close one he needed right then.

Jess snickered a welcome as he approached her. Soon she was dressed with saddle equipment and Hoffmann led her over to the pool where she drank her fill. The gunfighter swung up into leather once more, reined the horse back towards the trail and gently prodded the large horse's flanks.

The dead body of the young cowboy lay in awful repose at the bottom of the slate-grey escarpment. The only sound came from a gentle breeze and the buzzing of tiny wings from hungry flies that were swirling in profusion around his bloodied head. Hoffmann had collected the man's gelding from a scrub oak thicket on his way there and within ten minutes he rode off, with the body of the youngster draped over the jittery horse, secured at the cantle.

For an hour Hoffmann rode the horses downwards. The sun rose a little higher and he could feel heat beginning to return to the land. They came to prairie, mixed with outcrops of cottonwoods and mesquite. Then onward to see vast tracts of open prairie, rolling away into the far distance on the left, cacti here and there spotting the landscape. Flat-lands that were fluid with the movement of tumbleweed and dust, under buttermilk skies. The trail led upwards once more and towards high, rocky hills, where the small mining town of Oaksville was situated.

The gunfighter realised that someone from Indian Wells must have ridden the High Peaks Trail in front of him, and given the warning of his approach. No telegraph lines ran to a backwater like Oaksville. True, Hoffmann was taking a leisurely ride there, but even so, a good horseman must have ridden like the wind to do it, because the young cowboy bushwhacker had been there ready and waiting for him on the trail, after at least a two-hour ride out from Oaksville.

Unless members of the Indian Wells Citizens' Committee had talked, which was possible, no one apart from Sourdough would have known where he was going. Hoffmann mused on whether the secret fast rider was one of the committee, but could come to no conclusion.

Such was the gunfighter's early rise that morning, the occupants of Oaksville had hardly rubbed their collective eyes open, when he rode into their sleepy little town.

'I want yuh to bury a man for me, soon as possible.'

The owner of the funeral parlour, barely with sleep out of his eyes, looked back at the stranger standing in the doorway before him.

'Where is he?'

'Tied over his horse, outside.' Hoffmann was standing tall and lean. Trail dust still caked to his clothes. He looked strangely forbidding. 'The fella tried to drygulch me back up the High Peaks Trail. Got some money to pay yuh. What's the charge?'

The man gathered his wits some. 'Well, that depends on just what you want, stranger. Our top o' the range, all in...'

'Found twenty dollars and a battered watch in his saddle-boot. Yuh can have his nag as well.' Hoffmann dropped the money and watch on top of a coffin stand. 'Enough? 'Cos if it ain't, I'll dig a hole right here outside yuh shop and drop him in. The cowson owes me no favours.'

The undertaker's long, sallow face didn't show any reaction. He had buried a lot of men for a lot of different reasons and it didn't pay to query twenty dollars and a horse. Especially where no mourners would be involved and no questions asked. And especially with someone toting hardware like that. 'Sure Mister... Didn't get your name?'

'Grateful to yuh. Someone help me in with the fella before he stinks the street out?'

'Sure, sure.' The man moved to the door quickly and opened it. 'Been dead long?'

'Last night.'

'Hmm. Sun'll be high pretty soon. We'd best get him in out the back. Got fluids which'll sort that out.'

They untied the body, and carried it inside the shop and then through to a mortuary. 'Quite a mess ain't he? What you hit him with – a tree trunk?'

Hoffmann shook his head. 'Fell off a cliff.'

The man wanted to ask more, but thought better of it.

'You know where I can get hold of a man called Joshua Soames?'

The undertaker's grey pallor suddenly looked even greyer. 'Soames? You know him?'

'Not exactly. Wanna speak to him. Can yuh tell me where I can find him?'

'Down the street, on the left. Big set o' brown clapboard buildings. Used to be owned by the mine, before they went broke. Joshua Soames and his friends use it as a base – come and go all the time.'

'A base for what?'

The undertaker shook his head, implying that he had said too much already. 'Don't know their business and I don't want to, mister. They puts quite a bit o' work my way, without me asking for trouble. Three men fell out with Soames and his buddies a while back. Something about money owed. I buried them a week before last. Just like you, they rode into town. Only difference was, there was three o' them. And you're only one!'

Hoffmann nodded. 'Obliged to yuh.'

The undertaker suddenly tapped his head with a bony forefinger. 'Hey. You say the body out back is of a fella who tried to bushwhack you? Thought I knew him from somewheres. Yeah. Youngster came into town a couple o' weeks ago, bragging how tough he was and how he wanted to be the best shootist in the territory. Name o' Spratt I think, something like that anyhow. I saw him working for Soames last week – pretty sure it was him.'

The dour man stopped talking and rubbed his face. He stared back at Hoffmann suddenly, with fear written into it. 'I figure you're a man who'll take no offence for being given some honest advice, mister. If you killed that young critter, for whatever reason, you'd best get out of this town now. Soames don't like folks who muscle in on him. And on your own you're as good as dead.'

The gunfighter nodded. 'Thanks for yuh advice. From what yuh tell me, this Soames sounds like he's a bully. And with bully-boys at his beckonin'. In my experience, Mister Undertaker, bully-boys are deep-down cowards, running scared of something. Could be Soames has got a tiger by the tail an' he can't let go. Whatever it is, I'd bet my boots that he's mighty scared of something we don't know about and I aim to find out just what that something is.'

The funeral parlour owner stared after the

stranger in silence as he left his shop. It was an unpleasant situation. He did not want to get any more involved and rubbing his face once more, he turned around and entered the mortuary.

Outside, Hoffmann stood looking up the street in the direction of the mine buildings. He turned, patted Jess and mounted the horse. The sun was up now, burning away the early coolness and raising a faint, fresh smell from the dew-wetted ground. Birds were singing, a dog started yelping and somewhere behind him a cock crowed. The town was coming awake, a few people were already out, sweeping the boardwalks in front of their stores and a wagon full of lumber was rolling slowly into town.

Jack Hoffmann nudged the mare's flanks and rode slowly along the street. Soon the clapboard buildings appeared to his left. They were in poor repair, set around a large rectangle of land, with hitching rails out front of each hut. Leaning against one of the rails was a big, ugly man in his early thirties. He wore an open buffalo coat over greasy dungarees with a bib front and a dirty stetson pushed back on his head.

He watched Hoffmann, casually at first. A dark man, with jet-black hair, on a large roan mare. The man looked closer and he realised that the stranger was heading for the mine quadrangle. He suddenly felt fear prickle unaccountably at the nape of his neck, an irrational fear at first until he saw the short scattergun rocking gently against leather chaps. The ugly man had never met Jack Hoffmann before, but the bounty hunter's name suddenly fell from his lips in a frightened whisper. He watched him pull up directly in front and climb down from the horse. Dark man, with dark eyes. Looking into them was like seeing pools of death. He stood so close now. The man could feel Hoffmann's breath on his ugly face. A face that was reflecting the unaccountable terror he felt inside.

'Your name Soames?' The words came out slow, with a velvet feel in the cadence, like the deep growl of a cougar. 'Yuh hear me, boy?'

The man shook his head, eyes staring back like a terror-stricken animal before the kill.

'I've come for Soames. Now you take me to him, nice an' gentle like, or I'll blow your arse through your goddamn head!'

The ugly man backed off and raised his hands as Hoffmann slowly drew his Peacemaker.

'OK. Soames is through in the ore washery with the others.' He pointed across to his left.

The gunfighter turned, pushing the muzzle of his cocked revolver into the back of the big man and they entered through the creaking, board door that he had indicated.

FOUR

The ore washery was in the largest of the huts. It was long, with an opening at the back from where small ore cars used to run on steel rails up to the mine output tunnel. Beside the rails a hard-packed dirt path had been created. Mules once laboured there, pulling the heavy cars up the incline after they had emptied their load. Some years of disuse had allowed the trackway to become filled with weeds and as Hoffmann entered with his prisoner, he could see the tanks and other equipment used for washing and grading gold ore from the rubbish in rusty, almost unusable condition. He prompted the big man with the muzzle of the Colt. They moved forward to a large partitioned room with the door missing from its hinges. Inside, five men were sitting at a round, battered table playing cards. Three of them on the far side suddenly realised the danger, stood up and started to reach for their side arms.

Jack Hoffmann pushed his prisoner and

the man tottered across the room. The Colt revolver was already in Hoffmann's left hand and he swung the scattergun out from its purpose-made holster, cross-draw style, so quickly that the others were taken utterly by surprise. His words were curt and held authority. 'Move a muscle an' yuh all be dead men.' He paused and looked around. 'Yuh all seen how quick ol' "Betsy" here can be; the Peacemaker's much quicker. Believe me.' With easy actions, he dropped the Colt back into its holster on his right hip with his left hand.

'What the hell d'ya think ya doing on mah property?' The words came from a tough, muscular individual with a broken nose, set in what once must have been a handsome face. He was in his late thirties, standing at the other side of the table, directly opposite Hoffmann. He had thick brown hair and a full moustache that drooped over the ends of a wide, cruel mouth. The gunfighter could see that the hard case was just itching to let fly with the gun tied down on his left hip, an ivory handled Dance revolver, protruding from under the bottom of his old tasselled jacket. The gun was clearly ready and used regularly in action.

The other men started to move slowly,

turning around and trying to position them-selves to best advantage. Hoffmann cradled the cut-down scattergun in both hands with the ease of someone very used to working with the unusual weapon. Living the life he had for many hard years had honed his instincts for men such as these, to a fine pitch. Time and again he wondered how some could be so very stupid. Out of the corner of his eye he watched a short, thin man on his right, still wearing a greasy stetson at the back of his head, suddenly go for his gun. Hoffmann was lightning quick.

The Peacemaker was in killing position nearly a second before the man had cleared leather and the explosion from a detonated shell-case in the semi-confined space of the room shook the gang from any notion of bravado. The thin man was smashed against the partition wall and back across the table by the force of impact, red worms of gut and intestines blown out of his lower back and spewed about the room from where the .45 calibre slug had exited. A red smear defaced the wall, smoke wreathed the man's body and Hoffmann spoke a few seconds later – his voice holding a deep, precise cadence.

'I assume he is not Soames. I seem to kill a lot of men sometimes, before I gets to the one I want.' Silence filling the air, now changed to a coldness as if ice was there. 'I've come for Soames.' He looked at the hard man opposite, dark eyes locked on him. 'Yuh Joshua Soames?' The two stared at each other – neither giving anything.

'Yeah. I'm Soames. You're mighty handy with that gun. You've got the drop on me, stranger. Pity you don't let us even things up some.' The body on the table kicked a death throe, blood trickled out of the corner of a white-lipped, open mouth, and the dead man fell to the floor with a dull thud.

'Well, yuh've had six to one and yuh ain't done so well with that. Yuh figurin' five to one is just too dangerous for yuh?'

The gang leader could see contempt for him in the gunfighter's eyes, which were locked to his once more. Black orbs of death. He shuddered inwardly. Soames was no one's fool. He just needed some time. In the back would be the best way for this one, if he could only get the chance.

'Didn't get your name, mister? What you want with me?'

'There's a bad smell in here.' Hoffmann indicated over his shoulder. 'You boys all move out and line up in front of that ore trough, nice an' slow now.'

The five did as they were told and stood with their backs against a long, high lumber construction used for filtering gold ore, which was set among other equipment inside the large building. Soames repeated his question.

'The name's Jack Hoffmann. And I'm looking for the whereabouts of a man called Daniel Mackenzie. Been told you fellas can tell me where he's gone to.'

'Wal, I wonder who told yer that? That all yer want?' Soames grinned. False friendship suddenly in his features. 'Sure I kin tell yer the bit I knows about him, Mister Hoffmann. Young fella. Sassy accent. Came from out east, so he told me. Just a passin' through a mite, on a western trip, he said. Looking for the feel o' the West. For his pa it wuz, a big man back east so's I gather. Dunno what, but I figure a business man or somethin'. Maybe he wants to head up a cattle ranch. That's all I knows. And that's the truth on it. Now hows about us all settin' down a mite fer a drink? All thisn talkin's done made me dry. Whadda yer say Mister Hoffmann?'

Jack Hoffmann wasn't being fooled for one moment by the sudden change of heart. His eyes burned back, yet a thin smile flickered on his lips.

'That's mighty nice o' yuh Mister Soames.' He carefully lowered "Betsy," holstered it and the Colt. 'If you're willin' to sit down and talk this thing through a while, then so am I.' Hoffmann turned his back on them slowly, as if to make for the room; his eyes, ears and every sense at breaking point for any indication of sudden movement.

'Now!' Joshua Soames' guttural voice barked out the command to his henchmen and before the word had fully left his mouth, Hoffmann was turning through the air, the Peacemaker cleared of leather as he hit the floor. The palm of his left hand fanned the hammer. The Colt broke forth fire, lead and smoke, and two men fell dead against the lumber side of the ore trough in an instant of blood and mayhem. Soames was as quick with a revolver as he had looked and he loosed off two slugs at Hoffmann, which winged past, so close that he felt the heat from their passage as he dived behind a large sheet iron settlement tank. Soames assayed a couple more shots at the heavy, water-filled tank in the area where he thought the gunfighter to be hidden. Surprisingly, the iron sides dented from impact but the slugs were deflected from entry. Then all went deathly silent.

And then there were three. Hoffmann ejected two spent cartridges and reloaded. He may have killed two of the robbers but he also realised the peril of his position now. Three men clearly afforded a pincer movement for any tactician with the simple animal cunning of Soames. He noticed a small recess in the straight side of the tank where an inspection ladder was mounted. Hoffmann checked around and then moved himself into it; now out of the direct line of fire from anyone assaying shots randomly along the space, he relaxed slightly. Feeling cold rungs of steel pressing hard against his neck the gunfighter was aware of cold sweat on his back. Carefully, he listened. Only the intermittent sound of dripping water came to his ears. Not a living thing stirred in that building for a good two minutes.

A partition wall ran alongside the settlement tank. It created an alleyway about four feet wide that restricted him to only two routes of escape – either direction along the side of the tank. Almost imperceptibly now, he became aware of movement from behind the thin wall. Anyone who was behind that wall and hurled lead from a couple of revolvers blindly in his general direction, would be in with a good chance of scoring. And someone was there! The bounty hunter felt himself go cold. He was almost a sitting target!

Holstering the Peacemaker, Jack Hoffmann took out 'Betsy' and quietly cocked the scattergun. It felt good. Back up! Thanks Dwight. I remember all that yuh taught.

He wanted the greatest spread of fire and the only way to achieve it was with his back against the ladder. Hoffmann stood totally still, every sense that he bore utterly committed to sensing his adversary. He waited. Then the time of instinct and sensing came. A massive detonation from the ten-gauge shotgun blew a fire ball from the gun's muzzle. Instantly, red-hot shot tore a ragged hole of splinters through the wall that could almost be stepped through. Terrible screams issued from the splintered mess, saying everything, and Hoffmann put two slugs from the Colt through the partition, one either side of the ragged opening. Silence came once more.

Then there were two! He ran, controlled instincts guiding him now, along the narrow passage. At the end of the long settlement tank was an open space between two piles of heavy wooded caskets. He dived through the gap and rolled into the opening of a small, poorly lit room. As he did so, the bark of a Colt sounded and a slug narrowly missed his back. The form of a large man moved quickly in the corner and the space was illuminated once more with the bright light of gun-fire. Before his assailant could shoot again, Jack Hoffmann had turned and fanned the Colt. In the brief, awful light of his own gun-fire, Hoffmann saw the big, ugly man in his buffalo coat set out in relief against the wall. Then he watched him turn and slowly fall to the dirt floor, a large defacemen filling the back of the coat, like solidifying crimson lava.

And then there was one! Sudden movement outside the small room caused the gunfighter to roll over and he saw the fleeting figure of Soames disappear through the opening at the back of the hut where the track-way ran up to the mine. He rose to his feet quickly and ran across to see the gang leader scurrying from cover to cover, until he eventually vanished into the tunnel entrance of the mine. Soames had lost every member of his gang of cut-throats, to one man. But he had also lost something else, something of much more value to an outlaw – his reputation. A man's rep, in his line of business, out West, could equate to existence itself.

The gunfighter decided to leave Soames in the old mine for a while and search the ore washery as his first task for anything that could help reveal the whereabouts of Dan Mackenzie. This decided upon, Hoffmann returned to the room where he had shot the first robber. A careful investigation of everything, including the contents of the man's pockets, revealed nothing. After searching further, he noticed a door on the other side of the hut, behind the long ore trough. It was like a cupboard door set into the wall but heavily reinforced. A try at the handle showed it to be locked. Two shots from the Colt saw the lock blown to pieces. He reloaded the revolver carefully and also the scattergun, then pulled at the door. It remained firmly shut! The impact of the bullets had jammed the lock into its catchment plate in the door frame. The gunfighter looked around for anything which might help him and a five minute search revealed a hooked, steel jemmy which could tip the balance in forcing entry. Hoffmann got a fair purchase between the frame and the door gap, used all of his great strength, but to no avail. Soames sure made a good job of reinforcing that door, he decided and looked for something to give him the edge. Within seconds he had found it. A long piece of pipe slid over the end of the jemmy and increased its effective length by some four feet. He strained every muscle in his body and the sound of splintering oak burst across the old building like a rifle crack as the lock broke free and the door suddenly swung wide open across the passage.

Inside, the hidden space proved indeed to be a cupboard, filled with shelves large enough for even a man as tall as Jack Hoffmann to walk into. And upon those shelves the bounty hunter found more booty than he had seen in a very long while. Dollar bills in piles, gold bracelets, rings, necklaces, earrings, jewellery of all sorts and, stowed in the corner under one of the shelves was a heavy, iron-bound trunk, the lock blown away. The scratched surface had wording upon it. He could see clearly the stencilled lettering: 'Wells Fargo. Denver, Colorado.' Absolute proof that these men were the robbers he had known them to be. And stage-coach robbers at that!

The gunfighter decided Soames must be a most punctilious individual, in spite of his appearance, for everything was placed in careful piles, according to type; as if he had stood in that tiny space for hours on end, counting, organizing and filing his ill-gotten gains into sense and order with malicious pleasure. Whilst sifting through the rings, Hoffmann found a man's large gold signet ring with the engraved letters. D.G.M. Daniel – something – Mackenzie, perhaps? Hoffmann knew the President's Christian name was Grover. What more likely a second name for a beloved only son than that of his father – Grover? The tall man put the ring into an inside pocket of his buckskin jacket and shut the door of the cupboard.

Now for Joshua Soames! As Hoffmann walked over to the rail track running up the hillside, his eyes took on their hard, deadly hue. The gunfighter knew the odds on bringing out the man alive were very slight. The only safe way would be to starve him out – and that would take far too long. He started climbing well to one side of the rails, away from the direct fire of anyone laying down a volley from the entrance. He held the Colt in firing position, watched out for any sign of danger and continued upwards, conscious of his vulnerability.

Half-way up the talus petered out and he was pleased to feel firm rock and packed earth under his feet. Gorse and brushwood clung in spasmodic clumps higher up and a jack rabbit sprinted by just in front. The mine was set in a jutting portion of the mountainside, deeply notched between two summits. A quick look back down the scant path surprised him. Gun-fire from the encounter had apparently aroused the inhabitants of Oaksville from their slumbers and a fair number of people were now watching events progress from first floor windows, high vantage points and even roofs. He entered the cave slowly, making each footfall as quiet as possible and looking out for any sign of a boulder or recess that would afford some cover. None could be seen. A pencil beam of natural light lay ahead, which he discovered was coming from an open fissure in the mountain, going from the cave ceiling to daylight high above.

A little beyond this tiny, vertical chimney, the fairly wide tunnel opened out further into a large gallery. Two smaller tunnels ran from the gallery, one sharply to the left and the other, more or less straight ahead. Hoffmann could see enough to make out the shape of one of the old railcars standing out of use against the gallery wall. It was clear how the miners utilised the heaving iron-clad carriages to take ore down the very steep incline to the washery shed. A large, ratchet-operated hand-brake was mounted to the truck's side and judicious adjustment of the lever, according to the degree of slope, allowed the ore-filled carriages to descend down the mountainside, in a controlled fashion. Hoffmann was fairly certain that the man was not hiding in the car, because anyone would be a sitting target there, once his position was given away by the first salvo.

No. For a cunning man like Soames to enter this underground cavern of his own free will, it was pretty certain that he must know something. A plan perhaps that would offer a very good chance of killing Jack Hoffmann outright.

The gang leader lay in a tiny hideaway above the tunnel roof, listening intently for any movement below. Joshua Soames had seen his foe climbing up the hillside towards him and then returned to his safe cover, like a spider awaiting a fly. The robber watched Hoffmann pass underneath from the relative safety of the chimney and listened carefully to quiet footsteps as they faded into the gloom of the mine. The greatest danger and risk now lay ahead, at the beginning of an outrageous trap he had set for Hoffmann.

The springing of it, he hoped, would soon deal for good with this man he had quickly learned to hate.

A rope secured high up in the fissure years before to allow escape if the cave entrance ever became blocked whilst miners were at their labours, was the key to his plan. Soames was slim and still agile for his age. He lowered himself in silence, slowly descending into the chimney. Within a short time his feet became freed from the confines of the narrow fissure, then his torso and finally the robber got a good look beneath his hiding place and into the tunnel itself. Momentarily, he was taken by total surprise and froze on the rope in horror. For, no more than thirty yards ahead, the gunfighter stood surveying the gallery and looking over the old railcar which had been abandoned against the cave wall.

Soames held his breath and slowly slid the short distance to the floor. Then with Hoffmann's back still towards him, he pulled out a revolver and cocked it. In that split-second Jack Hoffmann reacted like lightning to the sound, which in such a dark, desolate place of deep silences, sounded like a rifle crack. The robber's six-gun was in killing position and Hoffmann's sudden movement preceded the gun's discharge by a hair's breadth of time. The loud bark instantly shook the whole mine and the hurtling slug of burning lead clipped Hoffmann's head with such ferocity that he was thrown sideways against the railcar, as if struck a heavy and direct blow by a large man. He then fell to the ground almost unconscious and lay completely still. Soames grinned at the sight. He was convinced that his foe was dead, or at the very least out of action for a long while. Long enough to put the second part of his plan into operation and finalise the matter conclusively. He would remove the hoard of money he had hidden in the mine and dynamite the roof, trapping Hoffmann in the bowels of the earth for ever.

The bullet wound had been a close call. Far too close. Hoffmann cursed himself for the slip. Many years of living on his wits had honed physical and mental faculties to a fine pitch and soon he was stable again and made a conscious effort to remain completely still. Partially dazed, Hoffmann scanned the limits of his vision, but could see no one. He took the opportunity of drawing his Peacemaker and bringing it up beside him to save time if a chance did occur.

The route out of there, through the only

entrance and on to comparative safety, was just out of sight around a bend, at some eighty yards' distance from where he lay. Hoffmann heard a rumbling of iron wheels on rails to his right and watched Soames appear out of the smaller tunnel pushing one of the ore cars along the narrow gauge track-way, with much effort. He pulled on the hand-brake and returned once more into the tunnel, disappearing out of Hoffmann's sight.

Slowly, with much effort, Soames walked the distance from some hidden store to the truck, carrying silver-coloured hessian sacks, which he threw inside. He made the journey five times. On the final trip, the robber carried a bundle of dynamite – Hoffmann figured about six sticks – enough to blow the whole mine entrance down.

The robber climbed on to the railcar, his back to the mine entrance, and looked directly at the indistinct form of Jack Hoffmann, lying completely still in the shadows of the gallery. A wide leer appeared across the man's broad face, his bushy moustache and thick brown hair giving him, in that half-light the classic appearance of so many bad men on a thousand wanted posters. The tassels from the bottom of his jacket and at the arms, looked almost black in near silhouette from the brighter light behind. The dynamite bundle was in his left hand and he tossed it gently up and down.

'Wal, it's time to say goodbye friend. Yer may have been the best sonofabitch gunslick I've ever clapped eyes on, but yer just ain't smart enough: 'cos you're dead.' He took out a handful of assorted dollar bills from one of the silver bags, singles, fives and tens and shook them. 'There's over $52,000 here. Speed ain't everything sucker – yer gotta have brains too!'

Soames grasped the long brake lever and released it. Slowly the heavy carriage started to roll back down the line. He reset the lever part way to control the descent, took out a red-head and struck it on the side of the truck. 'So long sucker!'

The gunfighter carefully lifted his Peacemaker out from beind the old railcar, raised himself a little for aiming and levelled the gun's muzzle towards his prey. As he did so, his head suddenly swam from the exertion and good vision quickly blurred into a sea of indistinction.

'Yer just needed some more brains, friend.' The robber lit the dynamite's fuse and as he tossed the still lighted match over the side, a shattering gunshot rent the air. Instantly, Soames was thrown backwards and spun round by the force of Hoffmann's .45 slug, which entered his left shoulder and blew part of his clavicle away. The bundle of dynamite fell from his hand and into the truck body, a thin trail of smoke waving up from the burning fuse. Somehow the man got to his feet among bags of his ill-gotten gains, eyes alight with a mixture of pain, fury and fear. He swayed forward on to the brake lever and tried to master himself. The effort was abortive. As he fell once more, passing into oblivion, his hand grasped the lever for support. The fast clicking of pawls on the ratchet witnessed the hand-brake's full and sudden release as the lever moved through its arc of movement. Soames disappeared inside the ore car, except for his arm, which remained hanging over the side, swinging limply to and fro in a sort of grotesque farewell. The laden truck started to gather speed and rumbled heavily towards the mouth of the tunnel, leaving a thin trail of white smoke from the burning fuse curling behind it.

Jack Hoffmann rose to his feet and ran forward with every bit of strength he could summon. If the fuse lasted long enough for the truck to exit the tunnel and him to get clear, he would be relatively safe from the explosion. There were two more simple options. One was acceptable, the other not. A premature detonation with Hoffmann running directly behind the ore car, would be a quick, painless end. If he tired and the tunnel entrance was brought down, a slow death awaited him, trapped in darkness.

The eighty-yard sprint was the hardest he had ever undertaken in his life. Brilliant sunshine poured over and filled the gun-fighter's senses as he emerged from the black cavern with his head swimming and watched the ore truck rattling away down the hillside. He staggered to one side and leant against the rock face, temporarily drained by his efforts.

The wooden frontier buildings of Oaksville lay behind the sprawl of sheds at the bottom of the slope. Every single inhabitant of the town now seemed to be watching events that had been started by him little more than an hour before. They were crammed into every vantage point it was possible to find.

'The car's really travellin' now.'

'He's gettin' out of the truck – look! Soames is gettin' out!' Cries from others in the crowd could be heard above the rumbling wheels. A woman screamed from one of the upstairs windows and a roar of excitement quickly rose as the robber started to fight for his life. He was at the point of nearly jumping out, when a jolt from the hurtling railcar threw him off balance and back on to the silver bags of dollar bills. The truck came to the end of the rails and took out the buffers with effortless ease, the rotted lumber posts being of no use whatsoever now in stopping the runaway. A massive explosion then rent the air with such force that Hoffmann was knocked from his feet. It destroyed most of the washery shed in a blinding, orange flash, hurling pieces of roof, clapboard, pipe, sheets of iron, pallets, rocks, and all sorts of rubbish high into the air. Out of the stunned silence that held Oaksville, came a loud cry: 'Look – money. There's thousands of dollars, all a-comin' down!'

Jack Hoffmann shielded his eyes from the sun and looked up. Blackened bundles were turning and breaking into pieces among the falling debris, spilling confetti-like clouds widely in every direction. The remnants of $52,000 in single, five and ten denominations, were being blown to the four winds!

FIVE

Never before had any frontier town seen such sights. Cowboys, miners, bartenders, storekeepers, gamblers, saloon girls, pillars from every corner of that small society, were all out scurrying up and down collecting, as it seemed to them, money from heaven! Each and every street seemed to contain some windfall. Townsfolk were on roofs, balconies, out in gardens, in the lumber yard and corral, collecting with anything they could lay their hands on quickly. Sacks, boxes, even butterfly nets were pressed into service. Mr Lawson of the ironmonger's store was doing a roaring trade selling butterfly nets, until he realised that he could make much more money by collecting, rather than selling. The unscrupulous could have had a field day with so many unattended shops, houses and saloons, but they were out collecting too.

A gentle southerly wind picked up and was taking most of the money away from the hillside and out over the town. Hoffmann sat a little down from the mine entrance, twisted up a quirley and lit up. The tobacco tasted good and helped him regain himself as the sounds of joyous entertainment drifted across the hill. He could see a group of three or four whooping cowboys galloping up and down Main Street, each holding a large butterfly net high above their heads. Soon the money was all down, they dismounted, and with equal fervour started to pick up what they could from the ground and cram it into the nets.

The bounty hunter got to his feet and walked diagonally down and across the hillside, collecting dollar bills where he could. He crossed the rail track, taking a direct path to his horse, which, although hitched some distance from the point of explosion, was giving him some cause for concern. It was in this last area on the lower slopes that he found most of the money. A quick count afterwards revealed $112 all told. He stuffed the bills into pockets of his buckskin jacket and walked through some debris near the far end of the washery shed, which was amazingly still standing.

On the other side he found Jess, still there where he had tied her and apparently unharmed by events. She was jittery though. 'Quiet Jess, quiet now, girl.' He patted the animal and talked her into a calmer state with a soft gentle tone to his voice.

Behind him was Main Street, near to the town's entrance, and people were still to be seen everywhere noisily about the serious business of collecting the remains of the robbers' loot with absolute joy. It had taken the gang many years to accrue a great deal of wealth through robbery, extortion and violence. The townsfolk and visitors to Oaksville were now delighted for the opportunity of redressing the balance. The destruction of Soames' evil gang had, in a very great sense, liberated the town. The robbers had taken over the mine and closed it down to use as a storage base, regrouping there and making further plans for sorties of mayhem all over the territory. All of Oaksville had been rightfully terrified of them and their presence and stifled any growth of investment. It was quite clearly a dying town.

'Would you, sir, be the lawman who accounted for these scoundrels?'

Hoffmann turned around. Standing before him were two middle-aged men. One had a florid face, with silver coloured, pork-chop sideburns and clear blue eyes under a white, wide-brimmed, flat-crowned hat. He was dressed in a light grey, good quality suit, with a loud silk waistcoat. The other was a tall, thin individual with a bright enthusiastic face and small, urgent eyes. He wore a derby hat and a brown woollen suit also of good quality, but now beyond the better part of its long life. Dollar bills poked out of his left hip pocket and he was pushing them inside rather self-consciously, as Hoffmann turned.

The florid faced man continued in a confident manner. 'Sorry to disturb you, sir.' He looked at the absence of a star on Hoffmann's buckskin jacket, disappointment in his voice. 'I see that you ain't a law enforcement officer.'

The big man nodded. 'That's right.'

'It was you though – who did fer the gang?' interjected the thin man nodding expectantly, his prominent Adam's apple bobbing in an even thinner neck. 'Wasn't it?'

'Yeah. They started the gun-play.' Hoffmann looked back towards the carnage and then back at his questioners. 'And I was forced ta finish it!'

'Yer sure as heck did that mister!' The thin man grinned a wide, toothy smile and put out his hand. 'Yer sure did!'

Hoffmann took the firm handshake and then shook hands with the florid-faced man, who introduced himself as Jeremiah Wheeler.

'This here's Mister Albert Skinner,' he indicated to his companion, 'manager of the General Mercantile – this town's largest general trading company and leader in the latest goods from out east.'

Hoffmann acknowledged.

'And I'm manager of the Stockman's Bank,' the man continued. 'We are both proud to make your acquaintance, sir and would like to offer a hand of friendship to your good self, for all that you have just done for this here town.'

The bounty hunter nodded and wondered what was coming next.

Jeremiah Wheeler continued, 'Together with Herbert Reed, we formed a Citizens' Committee some time ago, in the absence of any law in these here parts. We're still too far out West to get an official, permanent peace officer and knowing that Soames and his hellish friends would take it personal like if we announced our intentions of setting up some kind of regulatory body, we have had to sit on our hands, so to speak, for all these years until a time when those damned thieves and footpads could be removed.

'I don't mind admitting to you, sir, that the town has gone right downhill since their arrival back in '82, not just socially, but financially as well.' Wheeler paused and wiped his neck with a large embroidered 'kerchief and continued, 'I 'spect you've guessed the drift I'm taking. We've got a good business proposition to put to you, sir. An easy chair beats a rocking saddle by a country mile, so we was wondering if you'd like to meet the Oaksville Citizens' Committee for luncheon, down at Mister Skinner's offices here, on the corner of Main and Bowdre, at midday? No commitment to you at all, sir, and the meal and drinks will all be compliments o' the town of Oaksville. We'd be mighty pleased if you'd accept!'

'Why thank yuh kindly Mister Wheeler and you also Mister Skinner. I'll be pleased to take up yuh offer.' Hoffmann removed his hat and wiped his brow. 'I want to be clear though, that I am already workin' for some folks at the moment, on a contract of the greatest urgency and am fully committed to it. A man who hires out his gun is always willing to talk business. That's the reality gentlemen. I'm a hired gun and a good one. If you're invitin' me to join with yuhselves and other law-abiding folks for lunch, yuh gotta accept that.'

Wheeler nodded. 'We do understand that Mister...?'

'Hoffmann.'

'Mister Hoffmann.' The banker's features held their serious look. 'But in times and places such as these, straight-actin' men come in many different guises. In my long life I've met lots o' strange characters. Some would rob you with a Colt revolver, others with a fountain pen. Often what looks like the best turns out to be the worst, if you gets mah meaning. I've learned to judge folks, not on what their appearance is, but what they do and how they do it – it's the only way.'

''Scuse me a-buttin' in an all, Jeremiah, but Mister Hoffmann's head looks like it could do with some attending to.' Albert Skinner pointed.

'Sure, sure. I was just a-coming to that, Albert.' He pondered for a moment. 'Mrs Anson over at the drug store near your place could fix him up, couldn't she?'

Skinner nodded. 'Sure could. Took some study fer doctorin' a while back, but had to pack it in an' return to Oaksville, on account o' the roof collapsin' in on her new frame house. Rebuilt it herself too. Mighty fine woman, mighty fine. She'll do yer a good job Mister Hoffmann.'

The gunfighter acknowledged. 'OK. I'll see her before meeting for yuh lunch offer. Got an important matter to put to rest first though. Would yuh two gents like to follow me?' Hoffmann opened the door where he had entered first thing that morning with the big, ugly robber and stepped inside what remained of the washery shed. The two townsmen followed him and among the devastation he pointed out the heavy cupboard door, where Soames had kept much of his loot.

Wheeler and Skinner looked staggered at the glittering contents when the door was opened. The array of gold, silver and precious artefacts inside had come through the explosion amazingly unscathed.

'Could you arrange for some trustworthy folks to transfer this to yuh bank vaults for safe keepin' until the marshal over in Cheyenne can sort matters out, Mister Wheeler? 'Cos folk are soon gonna discover this an' all. An' sticky fingers being what they are...'

'Certainly, certainly, Mister Hoffmann.' Jeremiah Wheeler turned to his awestruck companion. 'Some of your staff and mine. Tom Cutler is a sound fellow, and Mike Halladay...'

Hoffman started for the door. 'I'd best get over to see yuh Mrs Anson, gentlemen. Good day to yuh.'

The two men bade him good day excitedly and returned to their conversation with fervour.

By 11.15 Jack Hoffmann had Jess settled at a livery stables and found some clean accommodation, should he decide to stay longer. He had the wound on his head attended to, which appeared to be nothing really serious and stood on the corner of Main and Bowdre at twelve noon exactly, feeling clean and good. For a small mining town like Oaksville, the General Mercantile Trading Company looked a wealthy organisation. He entered the building and was soon directed upstairs, where a beaming Albert Skinner welcomed him warmly.

There were six men sitting around a big mahogany coffee table in easy chairs and smoking cigars. The gunfighter looked impressive as he strode into the ornate room – tall, slim and hard. He put his black stetson on a bentwood coat stand but kept the gun rig belted to his waist and for this reason declined the offer of a low arm chair to sit on, choosing an upright one, which he brought across to the gathering. His reputation had travelled far and wide in the territory west of Cheyenne and every one of the men gathered there had heard about the deadly guns Jack

Hoffmann wielded for a living.

They had a drink but discussed no business before luncheon, keeping talk mainly to friendly questioning about the bloody demise of Soames and his gang.

Talk got around to the reason for the gunfighter's visit to Oaksville. Two of the gathering remembered someone fitting Daniel's description tied to a horse and brought into the mine by some members of the gang two to three months ago. Also the youngster's escape, two days later. He had ridden in a northerly direction like the wind, so the story went, taking one of their best horses, and that alone had infuriated them. To the knowledge of both men, the unknown captive was never brought back to Oaksville. But Soames' number one, a man called Johnson, had returned alone some ten days later from a cow-town Hoffmann knew well, called Pine Ridge, with the big black stallion the escapee had used.

Jack Hoffmann had enjoyed his meal, the drinks and the company. Soon after the plates and empty glasses were removed, Jeremiah Wheeler made the formal business offer he had intimated earlier. The town needed a good enforcer to keep the rowdy elements in check, someone who could handle himself, a gun, and other men with reliability. There was also the promise of sheriff, a properly constituted position, subject to Hoffmann's performance over a period of a year or so. The gunfighter was pleased with the offer they had made, thanked Wheeler and the others and explained briefly about the contract he had to see through. Once it was completed, maybe something could be arranged between them. Afterwards, the company parted in good humour ... Hoffmann with the possibility of future work and the committee with a potential new and very effective sheriff.

He walked out onto the stoop of the General Mercantile, put on his black stetson and walked across the dusty road, churned and rutted by horse and wagon. He stepped up on to the boardwalk on the other side, taking long, purposeful strides among the throng of townspeople about their daily business. It was a good town; a place a man could settle some day – but not now, at least not for Jack Hoffmann. Some folks recognised him and gave friendly, if careful tidings of the day to the tall, dark man with a short, scatter gun at his left hip and a .45 Peacemaker on his right.

'Howdy, mister.'

'Good job yer did.'

'Mighty pleased to see ya, sir.'

The gunfighter acknowledged each and every greeting politely, spurs jingled and boots clumped the dusty boards as the big man walked with an easy, strong gait along Main towards the end of town.

He entered the livery stable and Jess snickered a welcome as Hoffmann neared her stall. He paid the hostler, dressed the horse with saddle equipment and led her outside to a water trough, where she drank her fill. Checking finally that everything was in place, the bounty hunter swung up into leather and reined Jess towards Oaksville's town entrance, gently prodding the horse's flanks. It was just after four in the afternoon and in late summer he could expect usable light for at least another five hours. Time enough to be well into the mountains *en route* to Pine Ridge, before making camp. Four hours saw him well up the trail, riding through arrays of pine and conifer trees. A little rain earlier had left a smell to the woodland that was both fresh and verdant. Rider and horse enjoyed the moment.

Jack Hoffman was contemplating his evening meal by camp-fire, when he and Jess rounded a bend and spotted a hooped wagon ahead of them with four mules in the shafts. It had been pulled up beside the trail and one of the rear wheels was off the axle. A woman stood there, almost silhouetted against the low sun, and next to her was an old man dressed in buckskins and a 'coonskin hat. The wiry old feller had his hands on his hips, enhancing an air of frustration to his general demeanour.

'Yuh look like yuh could do with a little help.'

The two turned in surprise as he rode up. 'Dad blame it. Well ifn it ain't mah old buddy, Jack Hoffmann. Mighty nice to see you, pilgrim. How'd yuh get on with Soames? Learn anything?'

'It's a long story, Sourdough.' Hoffmann gave a rare smile, revealing a row of white teeth, and leaned on the saddle horn. He was pleased at the meeting with the cussed old man for whom he had gained a grudging respect. 'Better tellin' round a camp-fire after some good vittles, I reckon.' The gunfighter's eyes smiled. His look strayed past Sourdough and to the woman.

The girl stood by the jockey box of the wagon staring up at his tall, range-hardened figure. She was dressed in a gingham blouse and a long riding skirt that reached down on to her polished black riding boots. A tasselled shawl, woven with a patterned relief, hung loosely around her shoulders. Hoffmann removed his hat, staring at her. She was worth staring at. Big blue eyes the colour of sky at sunrise were accentuated by long, dark lashes. Her full sensuous mouth, high cheekbones and small, button nose added to an air of overt sexuality that almost overwhelmed him.

Tresses of jet black hair fell neatly on to slim shoulders, contrasting vividly with the milk-white of her skin and to Jack Hoffmann there was a quality there beyond any measure of womanhood he had known. This powerful attraction was mixed with a special kind of cussedness that he could sense instinctively; a gutsy drive in the girl that comes rarely in any generation. She wore the light blue blouse unbuttoned at the neck due to the warmth of the late evening sun, and he could see her firm breasts swelling against the gingham. She clutched at the shawl, drawing it tightly around her as she saw his dark eyes resting upon her beauty.

'The wheel wuz screechin' an' came away too far when we tried ta git some grease into the hub.' The cackle of Sourdough's voice was like a barrel of rusty nails being emptied out and drew him from his reverie with a jolt. 'Can yuh lift the buck body, so's I kin git the wheel back on, pilgrim? I'd be mighty obliged.'

Hoffmann got down from the horse and tied the reins to a tree. 'Got the linchpin?'

'Yes, sir.'

The bounty hunter ducked down to peer at the axles and blocks they seemed solid enough to take the pounding of the rutted trail. 'Yuh pass me the wheel?' Sourdough did as he was asked and Hoffmann looked it over. All seemed to be sound and the hub centre had been well packed with grease. 'OK. When I lift, you be sure an' get the wheel on quickly.'

'Yes, sir.'

Hoffmann slid a grease bucket hanging from the rear axle to one end and as he stood up, found the woman standing with her back against the buck and her hands underneath it. 'Ma'am?' His voice reflected surprise.

'Two lift better than one.'

'Obliged to yuh ma'am.' He turned to Sourdough. 'Yuh ready?'

'Sure am, pilgrim.' The oldtimer spat out some tobacco and grinned, his blue eyes twinkling back from the craggy, white bearded face.

'OK, lift!'

The wagon creaked as it was drawn up and Sourdough showed himself to be as adept at the task as his many years in frontier country would imply. The iron-clad wheel went back on to the axle fairly easily and he quickly secured it with the linchpin.

'Thanks, Jack! Like I wuz a saying ta Mis Mackenzie here, we make a mighty fine team you an' me.'

'That so?' Hoffmann looked at the girl. 'Miss Mackenzie you say?'

'Sorry, pilgrim. Old Sourdough's forgettin' his manners. May I introduce you to Miss Bethan Mackenzie; Daniel's sister. She's come all this way out West ta look for him – agin her kin folks' wishes, as I understand it. Offered to drive this here old wagon to Pine Ridge for her. She's plum loco enough to have gone on her own – beggin' yuh pardon, ma'am. So I thought, what would mah old partner think ta that and old Sourdough made hisself available at once. Bethan, this here is mah good friend, Jack Hoffmann.'

The woman nodded. 'Mister Hoffmann.' Her voice was cool. 'You're a pistoleer, I take it? And searching for my brother for a one thousand dollar fee. Is that correct?'

'Plus expenses, paid monthly, ma'am. I

106

don't rightly see how you being out here in the wild is going to help matters none.'

He turned to the old man. 'Say, how come yuh a going to Pine Ridge?'

Sourdough grinned. 'Well ya see, pilgrim, I wuz up early on the morning ya left for Oaksville. Saw that eye-patch fella, Silas Smith, looking sort o' sly an' then sneak around the back of the bank. I followed after the critta jest as quiet as a field mouse an' saw him talkin' to some fella. Couldn't hear much, but seems they wuz known to each other. The other fella wuz called Harper; he'd a-come all the ways out from Pine Ridge ta see Silas Smith. They walked further down the alleyway as they chewed the cud some, an' I couldn't hear much more. Ol' eye-patch wuz pretty keyed up 'bout somethin' though. Couldn't tell what it wuz, but Harper agreed that he would ride out to Oaksville there an' then. Thought it could be to warn Soames about yooz a-goin' there to trace young Daniel! Couldn't be sure though. Smith called up to Harper as he mounted his horse for them ta meet afterwards at Pine Ridge. Said he would wait there fer a day or so, to git the nooz.

'I tried ta find ya, Jack. Honest! But by the time I routed back to the livery, yuh had up an' gone! Miss Bethan an' I talked it through an' figured yer could take care o' yuhself well enough. We couldn't get ta Oaksville in time anyways. And all things considered, it would be best for us to go on to Pine Ridge an' see what we could find! Ya don't blame me fer not warnin' yer, 'cos I wuz too slow – dad blame it – do yer, Jack?'

'That's OK, oldtimer.' Hoffmann's words were surprisingly matter-of-fact. 'Guess yuh did the right thing.'

He nodded and turned to Bethan. 'Sour-dough an' me have got a long trail ahead of us. Ifn we're gonna be successful in finding yuh brother, time is of the essence and, with the greatest respect, we can't afford to be slowed none.'

'By a woman?'

'Yes, ma'am. Good Book says some-wheres, that a man is worth two women, generally speakin' that is.'

'Generally speaking!' Bethan Mackenzie tossed her head back and laughed. 'Mister Hoffmann, your chauvinism is a credit to you. In the City of Washington there are men equally as bigoted as yourself. The trouble is, they hold sway over the fate of this great country of ours. Their ignorance requires some illumination and I hope time will educate them suitably. At least these primitive views that you hold do little harm out here in the backwoods. What are your coming plans to find my brother?'

Hoffmann's dark eyes bore back at the woman. He took off his dusty hat, banged it on his leg and indicated at the sun, now low on the horizon. 'Well Miss Mackenzie, first things first, I reckon. It'll be sundown soon. Ifn you were a real womanly sort o' gal, which yuh seemingly ain't, I'd say Sourdough an' me would settle the mules and horse down for the night and then make camp, whilst you go out for some kindlin' wood and make supper for yuh newly acquired menfolks. How about that? Or is that a little bit too beneath yuh city ways?'

Sourdough suddenly raised his hands and stood between them. 'It's gonna be dark soon, folks. Old Sourdough needs 'is beauty sleep, an' I figure you good folks do as well. Guess we'll all be a mite better off workin' rather than fightin'. Whata yer say?' The silence was sudden, heavy and brief.

Jack Hoffmann put the stetson back on his head. 'Yuh got a good point oldtimer.' He touched the rim. 'Sorry to give offence, ma'am – I talks pretty plain and no apologies for that. If we're all gonna get along – seems to me we're all gonna have to work at it some, figure?' He turned to Sourdough. 'I want yuh to drive the wagon down just short of that gully by the mesquites an' pull off the trail. We'll make camp up there, in the lee of those rocks.'

Sourdough nodded and climbed up on to the jockey box. 'You figure going on to Pine Ridge with us?'

''Bout the strength of it oldtimer. From what yuh bin tellin' me, I needs to talk some with that Silas Smith character. He should be there by now.'

'You be careful if you talk to that man; don't trust him.' Bethan's blue eyes blazed. 'He can talk his way around anything!'

'As you say ma'am. I'll be careful.' Hoffmann turned to Sourdough. 'Let's get movin', before the light goes.'

Bethan Mackenzie climbed up beside Sourdough and the bounty hunter looked up at her. 'Appreciate yuh collectin' some kindlin' wood an' settin' the fire a goin' up there, Miss Mackenzie. Perhaps yuh could get some vittles on the go as well, whilst yuh're about it, eh?' The tall man turned and strode away up the incline towards his horse, feeling the heat of her indignation burning like hot coals at the back of his neck.

SIX

The final rays of the sun cut lines of shimmering gold, greens and browns through the pine, cedar and oak-belted hills as it set beyond High Peaks Trail. Bethan Mackenzie looked out on the majestic beauty in silence. She stood on the far side of the wagon and away from the warmth of the camp-fire, feeling for a few brief moments, like a child seeing the world beyond its own doorway for the first time. The air had a tang of grass and sage, and all around her the wind in the trees was soughing its passage along the craggy rock faces like a mournful ghost.

She could hear the men sitting around the crackling fire behind her chatting quietly and the clank of cooking utensils as they emptied the last morsels of food on to their plates. Suddenly, the cry of a coyote cut through the night. The sound sped through the pines, a long and drawn-out howl that made her shiver and turn sharply, trying to judge its direction. The mournful wail felt like some awful premonition to her, full of foreboding, terribly empty and cold in the openness of that lonely night. Another, then another answered from the ridges and forested slopes around her. The eerie sound of the coyote's call, dug deep into the towns-woman's senses and she shivered again, turning back to the relative security of the camp. She walked across flower choked grasses, around the end of the wagon shafts and up into the gaze of two strong faces lit by the light of the fire.

'Mighty pretty up here, ain't it?'

Bethan swallowed her fear and nodded, answering truthfully. 'Yes it is.' She turned to Hoffmann who, like Sourdough was sitting on a three-legged oak stool close to the dancing flames of the fire. 'You said that after some food you would tell us about your meeting with those people in Oaksville and what you have found out about my brother.'

The gunfighter acknowledged. 'If yuh would like to set yuhself down by the fire, ma'am, I'll tell all I can. Time we all chewed the cud and made some plans for the future.' He got up, put her empty plate and mug into a bowl of water with the others and moved her stool nearer the fire. 'Set yuhself down Miss Mackenzie. I would like to talk to yuh both, in seriousness and in confidence.'

Bethan did as she was bid and Hoffmann settled down on his stool, rolling a quirley. Sourdough lit his corncob pipe from the fire and offered the burning brand to the bounty hunter, who lit his cigarette. The smell of tobacco smoke mixed with the familiar aroma of burning mesquite roots and branches on the camp-fire and silence fell on the small group as Hoffmann pushed his stetson to the back of his head.

'Soames is dead. The gang's finished and done with! The sons o' bitches had a young man held captive for two days before he escaped from them about two or three months ago. Sounds like he wuz yuh brother, ma'am.' The tall man got to his feet and took from his buckskin jacket the ring that had been among the hoard of jewellery back in the mine outbuilding. 'Yuh recognise this?' Gold facets shone brightly as he handed the girl the signet ring.

She looked up, astonishment in her face. 'Yes. It's Daniel's.'

'Dang me, Jack, if yer ain't gone an' found his trail.' The oldtimer jumped to his feet and bent over the ring, his blue eyes sparkling in the glow of the firelight. 'Do yer know where he went after he escaped?'

'Wal, that's the question, oldtimer.' The bounty hunter sat down on the stool and flicked ash at the fire. 'Nothin' definite. About ten days afterwards one o' the gang brought the horse back from Pine Ridge that Daniel had escaped on, that's why I wuz heading there. It's due north o' Oaksville and the nearest town. So it seems that Pine Ridge has some clues hidden away for us.' He paused and looked at Bethan. 'Can I ask yuh a straightforward question and what yuh might consider to be an impertinent one, Miss Mackenzie?'

The girl's beauty was accentuated by the gentle light from the blaze and the power of it suddenly caught Hoffmann unaware. She nodded a reply.

He pulled on the cigarette and looked into the fire. 'How does yuh brother get on with yuh folks? Is he a regular, home-lovin' sort o' fella? Or would he continue his fun out here, an' let them all stew just out of cussedness?' The big man raised his hand. 'Now the reason for this question is simple enough, ma'am. I've been a puzzling over somethin' mighty queer here, as yuh might say. Chances are, that once away from Soames an' his gang, he would have contacted yuh family back east – pronto. Stands to reason.

The fella had a bad fright. Folks would be a worrying an' all. And yet yuh brother's made no attempt to contact you or yuh folks. Is that correct?'

Bethan nodded. 'We've had no contact at all, as far as I know, and Daniel is, as you would put it, a regular sort of man. In fact, my brother is the most loving and kindly person I know. He would never leave us in suspense like this if he were free, I'm sure. The President has only two children, Daniel and myself. If anything, it is me who is the fire-brand, not him.'

Sourdough grinned. The tail of the 'coon-skin hat rested on his shoulder, the corncob was clenched between his teeth and poked out among the grizzled white of his beard. 'I kin rightly believe that, ma'am – beggin' yuh pardon, an' all!'

The young woman glared briefly and looked at Hoffmann, waiting for him to continue.

'It seems ta me, that this conspiracy is just a mite bigger than it first of all appears.' The gunfighter looked her strongly in the eye. 'Soames ain't the beginnin' an' end of it by a country mile, Miss Mackenzie. I think yuh gotta steel yuhself on that! Could be that someone else's picked up where that old renegade left off. An' the only realistic answer to that idea is to suggest someone knew of the escape soon after it happened, or darn well as near – someone in cahoots with Soames. Now I've learned enough about Joshua Soames to know he wouldn't share an opportunity with his own mother. Not unless that person was a-knowin' more than he did, an' a-payin' him somethin' pretty darned substantial.'

Sourdough's eyes brightened from out of his craggy face. 'Are ya saying that Soames wuz being hired by someone else to capture young Daniel – 'cos he wuz some bad ol' country boy, who could shoot? An' all on account o' this unknown fella knowin' Daniel Mackenize wuz the President's son?' The old man tapped the corncob on to the leg of the stool. 'Like a little ol' crawdad hiding in the corner of a pond, with somethin' much bigger a-swimming round?'

Hoffmann nodded. 'Yep. I guess so.'

Sourdough whistled and sat down. He pushed a spill into the fire and relit his pipe. 'Well I'll be doggone.'

Bethan picked up the coffee pot from the glowing embers at the edge of the fire. 'Coffee, gentlemen?' The frontiersmen accepted gratefully. She turned to the old man. 'I think your guess that Silas Smith sent this man Harper to warn the outlaws in Oaksville of Mister Hoffmann being on his way, is correct.' She looked down suddenly into the dancing flames of the fire and Hoffmann could see its reflection flickering in her lovely eyes. A bitter fury burned there.

'How's that, ma'am? Are yuh just talkin' woman's intuition, or yuh got anything at all we can work on?'

She passed the coffee around, settled herself back on the stool and took a sip from the steaming mug. 'My mother is dead and I am the only woman with any closeness to the President. It could be that a woman sees things differently when alone in much male company. I don't know, but I'm sure my brother Daniel and all the others allow Silas Smith much more power than he rightly deserves. I know him well. And I also know how cunning he can be. Like a fox, Mister Hoffmann.'

'So are yuh suggestin' Smith has master-minded yuh brother's abduction? And it wuz him who paid Soames?'

'I don't know.' Bethan glowered at the dark night. 'I don't see how he could have had direct, practical contact. Silas rarely leaves the President's suite of offices.'

'Shootin' down yuh own argument ain't yuh?'

Bethan thought for a moment and returned Hoffmann's stare. 'No. I don't think so. As I said, Silas is cunning. He wants power and wealth. If he can't have the former, he'll be only too pleased to make do with the latter. What better way to make a great deal of hard cash quickly, than to blackmail the President over his son?' She paused, sipped coffee and Hoffmann saw the fire burn again in her eyes. 'I'm pretty sure now that Silas Smith is clever and devious enough to have found a way!'

The gunfighter smiled grimly at her. 'Mebbe yuh right, ma'am.' He drained his mug and set it beside the stool. 'Miss Bethan – yuh don't mind me calling yuh Bethan...?'

'No. Not at all.'

'Well fact is, Bethan, I told yuh I wuz a plain speakin' man an' that's the best way I know to treat folks, all in all. So I'll be straight an' hope yuh takes no offence.'

He got up, refilled his mug, and offered coffee to the others. 'Fact is, life's not taught me much about understandin' womenfolk. I don't cotton to their ways o' thinkin' mostly, and that's the truth on it. 'Ceptin' for this intuition that gets itself up every now and then. Now in my experience, for what it's worth, I've found that a mighty powerful guide to the truth. Rarely lets a body down.

'I've found the way to make the best on it, is ta keep usin' yuh commonsense. Intuition might tell a fella there's gonna be a rainstorm. Maybe there's not a cloud in the sky, but he still feels it's gonna rain – in his bones yuh might say. He don't stay inside somewheres 'cos it might, but he still packs his slicker in the saddle boot afore ridin' out. Yuh gotta let intuition colour yuh commonsense, not dictate to it. Yuh sees my point?'

Bethan nodded. The fire crackled, logs near to ash collapsed in the middle of the blaze and Sourdough got up, throwing some more on the fire.

'Then it's clear what our next move should be. We'll all ride over to Pine Ridge an' confront Silas Smith – I'll see what can be got out o' him. We've got no proof against Smith, but something smells about this whole danged thing an' I don't like it! I'm also mindful of the fact that it is Silas Smith who is employing me with a fee of one thousand dollars if I succeed in a finding yuh brother. No one else. Ifn yuh right in what yuh say, I ain't a-gonna get paid, am I?' Hoffmann relit his cigarette. 'Now seeing as

I earn my livin' by bounty an' no other ta speak of and if Smith is the villain in this here piece, as he seems to be, it's not unreasonable of me to look for another source o' payment.' The bounty hunter's gaze moved from the blazing logs in front of him, to Bethan's clear blue eyes. "Cos as yuh can imagine, ma'am, I'm gonna be about as sore as a rattler stuck in a rain butt ifn I gets nothin' out o' this!'

The daughter of President Mackenzie held Hoffmann's stare firmly and challenged it – sudden anger in her face. 'That sounds awfully like a threat to me, Mister Hoffmann.'

'No, ma'am. It ain't meant to be. It's meant to be a statement of fact.' Jack Hoffmann's dark eyes narrowed from under the rim of his black stetson and to Bethan Mackenzie, he suddenly looked very dangerous. 'I'm promised a great deal of money by some eastern folks to do a very difficult job, for which I am qualified. Now as I look into the mess, it would seem the fella who's a-promised me the money might well be the culprit in the affair. He's taken me for a sucker and I'll have worked hard to bring my new employer to a probable hangin'! I ain't a-gonna get paid no thousand dollars for that, am I? Now for a little ol' country boy, that just don't sound like good business to me!'

'You're asking me to pay you one thousand dollars to free my brother?'

''Bout the strength of it Miss Mackenzie.'

'And if I'm wrong about Silas Smith and he is not the main villain, you'll threaten him for the money as well?'

Hoffmann shook his head slowly and laughed. The sound of it chilled her to the bone. 'Well dang me, ifn yuh ain't the most uppity, selfish young woman I's ever had the misfortune to come across.'

Bethan flared. 'Don't you dare speak to me like that!'

'Now, now, calm yuhself, ma'am.' He looked across to Sourdough who was puffing on the corncob and blinking at the two of them. 'Like I says. I don't rightly like dealin' with womenfolks – 'specially when it comes to business talk. Figure they got their heads a-full o' dresses an' cookin' an' all, to fully cotton to financial matters. The Good Lord made 'em best suited for lookin' after children an' tendin' ta the house an' vittles. An' we love 'em for it too.' He had a thin smile on his lips, knowing he was deliberately provoking her and enjoying it.

Bethan made to get up and found Sourdough's wiry arm suddenly on her shoulder. She caught his look and stayed seated. Fury was now surging through her like a river in full flood. No one had ever spoken to the President's daughter like this. Or even to her as an individual. Commonsense controlled the anger by only a very tiny margin. She was looking into the eyes of a professional killer.

'I only want paying for freein' yuh brother. No more an' no less than that. I don't care who pays me neither. Ifn Smith turns out ta be innocent, then I'll take his money as set by our agreement. Ifn he turnes out ta be the real kidnapper, as yuh suggest, then I'll want that thousand dollars from you, yuh kin, or anyone connected. Not fussy. Only want it. An' be clear on this Miss Mackenzie, I'll ride right up ta yuh President's House on ol' Jess there, an' in through the front door ta get mah money, ifn I's got to. People who owe me money always pay.'

Silence reigned as he looked into the simmering beauty of her whitened features. 'I'll want somethin' written out proper like, ink on paper, before I takes a further step on yourn behalf, or Daniel's. Yuh got ink and paper in that wagon?'

Bethan nodded. 'Yes. But I want to think about this first.'

He turned to Sourdough. 'Let's take a look at the horse an' mules before we settle down for the night, oldtimer.'

Sourdough nodded. 'Yes, sir.' He tapped the pipe out on the heel of his boot and got to his feet. 'Yer be all right Miss Bethan? Shan't be long.'

She nodded.

Hoffmann threw the butt of his quirley into the fire. 'If, whilst we're gone yuh decide to get that affidavit written, it'll be best done with and out o' the way.' He smiled, a rare and gentle smile, reserved usually for animals. 'I could collect it when we get back.'

'All right Mister Hoffmann, I'll do it because I love my brother and I think what you're asking is fair.' Her features glowed in the firelight and the gunfighter could see strength and courage shining from her eyes. 'I'm not frightened of you: don't for one minute think I've done it for that reason.'

He stood still. Tall and dark beside the blaze, then he touched the brim of his hat. 'Ma'am.' A coyote's cry cut across the clearing where they had camped, long and lonesome, and then a sudden whinny from Jess caught their attention. Hoffmann looked at the old man. 'She sounds a mite put out!' Sourdough picked up his ancient rifle that was leaning against the wagon wheel, both men then strode the distance to the chaparral thicket and vanished into the night, leaving Bethan alone.

She listened to the silence and another coyote's cry lifted out of the trees as she climbed up into the wagon. Bethan's hand was shaking a little as she lit a hurricane lamp and started writing.

Her formal offer to Jack Hoffmann was put into a envelope five minutes later. As she sealed the flap a shiver ran down her spine. The coyote had returned. Bethan disliked the mournful sound and wished the men would come back quickly. Soon, the cry ceased and silence filled the clearing once more. She got out of the wagon and stood by the fire, holding the envelope in her hand. She was now alone at night forty miles from the simplest form of civilisation, in one small part of the great expanse of Wyoming Territory, a piece of untamed country, not yet part of the Union. The only daughter of the President of the United States of America felt vulnerable and suddenly very alone.

The fire was burning low and she picked

up the last of the logs and threw them on. Sparks and the smell of burning mesquite lifted and then, stepping back, Bethan heard the sound. She looked ahead to where the bounty hunter and Sourdough had disappeared. For a moment her hopes rose. The sound came again: a crashing, a dragging through the bushes and trees. Something big. Then it stopped. She pushed the envelope into her belt and picked up a branch from the camp-fire; its end burst into light as she lifted the blazing brand high. Nothing could be seen at all. The townswoman turned slowly, wondering if the noise had misled her and suddenly the dragging sound came again, registering easily on her heightened senses, together with a deep, guttural and heavy growl. Bethan turned back, looking across the fire to the shadowy outlines of scrub oak trees on the far side. At the edge of the clearing she could see two yellowing eyes and the unmistakable shape of a great brown bear on all-fours, no more than eight yards away from her.

The gunfighter and the old man spun round together at the sound of the woman's scream. She was no more than fifty yards away from them in a straight line, but sounded a lot further. They started back as quickly as a dark night and lack of lantern-light allowed.

Bethan continued screaming for some moments and then pulled herself together, remaining frozen to the spot in sheer terror. It was too late. The shrill noise from the woman had alarmed and goaded the great bear and it rose on to its hind legs and moved towards her in a few great lumbering strides. In seconds, the enraged creature was towering over the terrified girl. It stood some six feet six inches in height – with only the dying glow of the camp-fire lying between them. Bethan moved one way and then the other, trying to avoid the huge white fangs she could see slavering at her in the firelight.

Suddenly, a shot rang out. Then another, bursting into a crescendo of blinding, bright light and thunderous noise. Bethan saw the creature drop back on to its forelegs, move away a little before she lost sight of it in the confusion of senses and fear, and fell to the ground.

She heard Jack Hoffmann's voice; a strong arm pulled her to her feet and Bethan found herself in his arms swathed in gunsmoke and crying uncontrollably against his broad shoulder.

'Hey now, ma'am. Yuh gonna get yuh face

all a-wet an' messed.' The big man cradled her in his arms and stroked her hair for two or three minutes before Sourdough returned.

'He's gone, Jack. Reckon it was the huckleberries he wuz after.'

Hoffmann nodded. 'Yeah.'

'Huckleberries?' Bethan pulled away from the big man and wiped her eyes.

'Yes, ma'am. Those old grizzlies love hucks. Hey. Stand over here on this side o' the fire.' Bethan walked over to Sourdough. He put his hands on her shoulders and gently turned her towards the wagon shafts. 'Now yuh take a good ol' lungful o' air, Miss Bethan. Yer smell anything?' She shook her head.

'Well the wind's in our direction and that ol' bear sure could. A grizzly can pick up the scent o' huckleberries at a quarter mile distance!'

'That's all he wuz after, ma'am – not you.'

Bethan shivered. 'If you have wounded him, he may be angry and come back. I've read that a wounded creature can be very dangerous.'

'He's not hurt none, Miss Bethan.' Sourdough's bright eyes twinkled.

Hoffmann was checking the Colt revolver. He looked up. 'That's right lady.'

Bethan's face held astonishment. 'But how can you be so sure?'

''Cos we didn't aim at him.' The gunfighter dropped the hand-gun back in his holster. 'Just scared him some!'

Her features changed from surprise to anger. 'You didn't aim at him? I was within inches of being torn to pieces by a huge grizzly bear and you did not aim at him?'

'No, Miss Bethan.' Hoffmann stooped down and raked the ashes of the fire and repositioned the logs. 'I knows yuh a mite upset, an' I kin understand that, what with yuh never having been really out of a city before, an' all. But things are different out here.' He shot her a glance. 'An' you've gotta learn ta change, more than some!'

Her voice was suddenly shrill. 'Change? What into Mister Hoffmann? A hillbilly?' She walked up to him. Five feet five, facing six feet one; utter fury written into every feature and her big blue eyes wide and tears welling. 'Why did you not shoot that ferocious animal? It was about to kill me? I thought killing was your profession. Why?' She bent down and picked up a heavy, unburnt stick that had rolled from the fire. In one sudden movement she raised it in her clenched fist and swung the piece of wood at his chest. The big man grabbed her wrist and took it from her gently.

'Now I could be wrong, but I don't think yuh really wanted to do that.' He dropped the stick back on to the ground. 'We did not kill that ol' bear, because he weren't out to hurt yuh at all. The reason he wuz on his big ol' hind legs an' growlin' so angry, wuz all down to you.'

The woman looked at him speechless. 'Me?'

'Yes, ma'am. That ol' grizzly wanted huckleberries. That's all. Bears are poor-sighted creatures. Don't make too much difference ta them whether it's night or day, 'cos they rely on smell an' hearin', in the main. He came a-lumberin' through his woods – not yours remember – an' hit our camp an' everythin'. All yuh had to do wuz to shout out to me an' Sourdough an' then keep outa his way. We'd have a come a-runnin'. But yuh screamin' out there like a banshee just frightened him first, then angered him so much that he upped at yuh.' He paused and let go of her arm. 'Just like yuh have been a-spittin' fire an hell at me. Yuh know how he feels now, don't yuh? We wouldn't shoot a body just 'cos they got a mite upset an' weren't gonna really do us harm. That wouldn't be fair or right. City folks kin see that just the same as us country folks.'

'You are treating that animal as if it were a human being.' Her face held puzzlement, anger and tears. 'You can't value the life of an animal on the same level as a human being – any human being!'

'No, ma'am. Like yuh say, he ain't human. But he deserves to live a lot more than some folks I know. I ain't no book read, clever man. I just knows who's out to kill me an' who ain't; man or beast. Or who's a gonna rob or cheat me, most times. That's why I'm still around. An' I would mightily suggest yuh start doing the same, ma'am. Ifn yuh want to survive out here in the frontier a decent spell.' Hoffmann was surprised when Bethan stood back and looked at him.

Her features had become hollow, wan and still. She spoke in a hoarse whisper as her wet eyes held his. 'Thank you, Mister Hoffmann. I will sleep on your words.' The shaken woman took the affidavit from her belt and handed it to him. She then turned and walked slowly towards the wagon.

'If we make an early start at sun-up, likely we'll reach Pine Ridge by late afternoon, mebbe sooner.'

Bethan nodded and climbed on to the wagon step. 'Right. I'll be up first thing. Good night to you both.'

As Bethan Mackenzie got into the buck, Hoffmann looked at Sourdough and the oldtimer smiled at him, then winked. The gunfighter was ill at ease with women. Yet somehow this one was different. She had brains, guts and something else that he could not quite fathom. Hoffmann smiled back at the old man and checked the fire, before they both laid out their bed-rolls by the wagon and retired for the night.

SEVEN

The party were up at dawn. They broke camp beneath the lee of the rocky outcrop as the sun rose in full splendour through distant, high cumulus clouds. The wagon with Bethan and Sourdough on board rumbled off along the rutted trail, which meandered slowly down from the high mountains. Beside them, on his big roan mare, the gunfighter rode in easy motion. The group passed through chaparral and mesquite clumps as they travelled, the bark and leaves shining with the wetness from a gentle rain shower that had started soon after dawn. In an hour the thickets of evergreen oak dispersed to reveal open prairie below.

Hoffmann's black stetson dripped. He wore a calf-length grey slicker wrapped around his legs, still shining with wetness from the rain that had followed the party down and was now disappearing with the first morning heat. Bethan and Sourdough had taken off their rain garb and were sitting on the box chatting. The old man had returned his 'coonskin hat to his head and the corncob was between his teeth as they lurched along; smoke drifted up, mixing with his garrulous, cheerful speech. He flicked the ribbons every now and then, tapping the leathers on the rear two mules and keeping the team of four at an even pace.

A further two hours saw them down on the flat expanse of prairie which stretched away to the horizon, an open sea of shimmering movement, fluid with dust and tumbleweed. The big, long-eared drag animals looked little troubled by the time spent on the trail since sun-up, even so, Hoffmann indicated to Sourdough to pull over and give everyone a short rest.

Soon, a distant rumbling rose on the air, dominating the windy silence and shaking the ground beneath the mules' and horse's feet. The party looked back to see a great herd of beeves crossing the range, flanked here and there by cowboys calling and whistling among clouds of prairie dust and the rolling thunder of many thousands of hooves.

'Get back on the wagon, Miss Bethan.' The gunfighter swung Jess in close to the buck. 'OK, Sourdough, move the wagon out. The herd will pass us in good time an' we're better off moving with them, than settin' still!'

Bethan had seen cattle being trailed from the safety of a railcar on her journey out into Wyoming Territory, but the reality of sitting on the pitching jockey box of their creaking range-wagon as the longhorns closed around, she found both exhilarating and terrifying. Sourdough gave whoops of glee as the thundering mass engulfed them: horns and hooves that were certain death to anyone who fell.

'Howdy there!'

They looked across in the direction of the shouted greeting to see a dust-caked rider astride a bay; leather chaps, a checked range shirt and a spotted bandanna barely definable among the jostling river of cattle and choking dust.

'Howdy!' Sourdough yelled back his reply, but the words were almost lost. 'Are yer driving to corral in Pine Ridge?'

'Yeah.' The sweat-soaked man moved his horse skilfully among the beasts and nearer to the wagon. 'You folks'll be jest fine set up there. We'll be past yuh in about twenty minutes – sit tight!' His voice carried across the multitude of longhorns thundering either side of the wagon, like a lamp-flame held up in a gale and in seconds he was gone.

135

'Yuh're doing fine Miss Bethan.' Jack Hoffmann shouted his encouragement to the girl and she responded.

'I'm OK, Mister Hoffmann.' Her words competed strongly with the uproar, but her reply had brightness in it. 'Now don't you go falling off that horse!'

'No, ma'am.' The big man touched the brim of his hat whilst correcting the jittery horse with leg and rein and gave a rare smile. The girl had spirit. For some time he had thought she had the makings of a frontierswoman in her and now could see it plainly.

They rumbled along, Sourdough gradually working the team of mules across to one side of the endless stream of cattle with yells and cheerful curses, so that they were driving alongside, rather than in among the thundering herd. Bethan's face shone with excitement as she watched cowboys chasing longhorns back into the great jostling stream. The 'yip-yip-yip' of range hands and the deep cries of the herd were a new music that fired the young woman's adrenalin.

The great herd eventually passed them and as the dust started to settle, the old man gave a cry. 'There she is, pilgrim, Pine Ridge – straight ahead o' us, through the dust cloud!' He turned to the gunfighter. 'Guess we made pretty good time, eh?'

Hoffmann pulled his bandanna from around his mouth, took off the dusty Stetson and wiped his brow. 'Reckon so, oldtimer. That herd o' beeves helped us along mighty fine!'

Pine Ridge was a rough, tough frontier cowtown. Civilisation was slowly reaching it though. In the last five years the outpost had gained in stature. The large, rougher elements had competition now and the upper strata of townsfolk boasted with pride of the Mercantile Trading Company in business there, three banks, a quality ladies outfitters, two eating establishments and a ladies' circle of Christian fellowship. Together with a businessmen's club, Citizens' Committee and three saloons, the town was set for a longterm prosperity. It was true the saloons had been there almost ever since the town had grown out of the dusty trail, but now, all three were under fairly stable ownership, often free of brawls for whole days, rather than hours. Nonetheless, the reason for the town's very existence was not lost on any of the population – cattle – the great herds were the town's life-blood and they knew it!

'Herd's a-comin' in! Herd's a-comin' in!'

The cry flew across the boardwalks into shops and up stairways. Small children were pulled from streets, merchandise quickly brought inside shops, horses taken to the back of buildings and windows that could open, were firmly closed.

The thunder of hooves and the bellowing of the great longhorns suddenly burst down on to Main, among dust and noise as the first of many thousands of dusty beeves turned at the top and ran between hitching rail, boardwalk and doorway. They were guided in their seemingly uncontrolled travel by yelling and whooping cowboys who were mounted on heavily lathered horses, man and beast struggling energetically towards the stock-yards and corrals set out in huge open areas across the town. The men, some as young as seventeen, waved hats, bandannas or lariats at the thundering mass, riding bravely among horn and hoof with a mixture of skill, confidence and hope, all thoughts turning now to what the outcome would be of this day's work as they approached their hard won destination at the cattle pens. Gradually the clamour and hubbub reduced as the herd was turned in. People returned excitedly to Main Street with their children, horses or shop goods and resumed everyday life as the remaining stragglers were driven past.

An hour later, when the last of the light brown trail dust had settled on roofs and roads, deputy Chas Clayton stuck his head around the door of the law-office. County Marshal Roy Cooder was sitting easily on a swivel chair, feet up at a battered, old-fashioned desk, reading a copy of the *Pine Ridge Gazette.* He was in his late forties, still of fairly slim build with long golden-white hair that rested generously on to the shoulders of his leather waistcoat. The man's moustache still had much of the blond colouring from his youth and it drooped over a strong, full-lipped mouth, under a hooked nose and worldly, slate grey eyes. He looked up casually and lowered the paper. 'Yeah?'

The deputy's long, dour face had nothing written on it. Only a possible hint of good spirits was betrayed there by a slight curl showing at the ends of his wide mouth. Cooder knew Chas Clayton well enough. The Texan was very pleased about something.

'Guess who I's a-got out here ta see yer, Marshal?' Clayton's slow drawl held a warmth of old friendships past. He stepped on to the room's bare floorboards, turned and put his hands on his hips, leaving the newcomer, a big man dressed in black, filling the doorway. Marshal Cooder threw the newspaper on to the desk and got to his feet with a broad smile spreading widely across his face.

'You old sonofabitch. How's yer doing, Jack?'

Hoffmann took off his stetson, ducked his head slightly and moved into the sparsely furnished law-office; the dark stained wood floor creaked to his movements. 'Mighty pleased ta see yuh again, Roy. Been a long time.'

'Too long.' The lawman's voice had a deep resonance to it like the growl from a big cougar. He turned to his deputy. 'Coffee's still hot in the pot, ain't it? Pour us all some will yuh Chas?'

Clayton nodded. He disappeared through a squeaking door that led out the back to the cells as Cooder bade the big man to sit down. He suddenly looked serious, benevolent almost.

'Yer should never have left, Jack. Soon after yer gave up the job o' sheriff, they elected me and then the job got made up to full federal marshal, on account o' the town growing with all the cattle business. Why did yer do it, boy? Sure as hell, you were a mighty good lawman.'

Hoffmann pulled up a rickety bentwood chair and it squeaked under his weight. He threw his dusty hat on to the desk. 'Got thuh wanderlust I guess.'

'An' Mary Jane?' Cooder's grey eyes held those of his old friend for some moments. 'She'd have been yourn wife by now.' He watched the bounty hunter as he looked across to three rifles held in a rack on the wall.

'Figured to find the bad men who killed her and settle matters – permanently.' His eyes met the marshal's stare strongly. 'Did that. Got the bounty money and sort o' drifted for a spell. My name got ta be known up in the Dakotas. Folks started looking me up for regulatory work – some fella would think himself tough and start a-pushin' for land rights or somethin'. Maybe he'd get together with his buddies to try an' hustle folks into their way o' thinkin', an' I'd get paid to kick some arses back in line.' A thin smile was on his lips.

'You had yourself some fun?'

'Yeah, I guess so. Got sort o' serious in the end, though. Woke up one morning and realised men were out to kill me – and on a serious basis. Not drink or temper talking. Made some enemies, Roy, as well as a lot o' good friends on the way. It was then it stopped being fun. My life was on the line. Like the old days when I was sheriff an' you was deputy. Took life an' bounty huntin' mighty serious after that.'

The gunfighter paused and his eyes drifted to the gun rack again. 'Sometimes when I kill a bad *hombre,* I'd see Mary Jane...'

The rear door squeaked open and Chas Clayton walked slowly into the room with two steaming mugs of black coffee. He put them on to the desk and looked at the big man.

'Sorry. I can't stop, Jack.' He indicated over his shoulder. 'Got ta catch the Lander stage before it pulls out.'

Roy Cooder nodded. 'Yeah, that's right.' He pulled open a drawer in his desk, took out an envelope and gave it to his deputy. 'Make sure that goes with the other mail will yuh, Chas?'

The Texan nodded. 'I'll see yuh around town, Jack.'

Hoffmann looked up. 'Mighty pleased. Be here for a few days I figure, Chas.'

The deputy's dour features altered slightly and for anyone who knew him, it revealed his pleasure. 'Yeah. We could talk a spell, later.' As Clayton closed the door leading on to the stoop behind him, the marshal took a swig of coffee and looked Hoffmann in the eye.

'Whata yer here for? Bounty?'

Hoffmann nodded. 'Private bounty to find the kidnapped son of the President of these here United States.'

Cooder's grey eyes widened. 'Yer a-kidding me, Jack?'

'No, I ain't. It is serious, Roy. A lot o' lives could be at stake.'

The marshal whistled.

Hoffmann got up and drank some of his coffee. 'You seen a thickset fella riding into town wearing an eye-patch? Goes by the name o' Silas Smith?'

Cooder's face was serious. 'Yeah. Do believe I have. 'Bout a couple of days ago. Rode in on a black. Lovely animal, with the best saddle this side o' the Rockies. The fella got money?'

'Mebbe. Leastways, I figure he could be trying to get himself some. Came here to meet a man called Harper. Local fella, so I'm told.'

Roy Cooder gestured with open hands. 'Lot o' Harpers in Pine Ridge. Don't know of a meetin' between yourn two, but I'll see what I kin find out, if you like?'

''Preciate that, Roy.' Hoffmann finished the last of his coffee and put the chair back.

'Tell yer what. Ol' Chas done told me that he'd seen that eye-patch fella headin' up the mountain trail towards Bill Thomas's place. He's got a spread in a valley up there, 'bout eight miles outa town. Might be worth yer riding over ta see Bill. Mark me, Jack, he's a funny sonofabitch. Had a bad time last winter. His herds were nearly wiped out. They say he's done gone broke – or near to it. So guess his short fuse temper'll be even shorter by now!'

Hoffmann nodded. 'Thanks, Roy. Might just do that! I'm staying with an oldtimer and a gal at Mrs O'Casey's rooming-house, near the Golden Garter. We'll all be over in the saloon later on, getting the dust out of our throats. ''Preciate you an' Chas joining us for a spell. Ifn yuh can make it?'

The marshal smiled. 'Sure. If things is quiet, we'll be over, Jack. Like old times.'

As Hoffmann closed the door behind him, he thought of the potential lead on Silas Smith and it cheered his spirits. Then of what might have been, had his earlier life in the cow-town taken a different route. He

144

also remembered Mary Jane and how she had been brutally gunned down by a panicky bank robber. Soon any regret at leaving his old job as sheriff of Pine Ridge passed, and he was walking down the familiar streets once more, acknowledging old acquaintances as he strode on. His strong gait, long legs and the dark aura surrounding his tall, range-hardened figure had an effect on all who saw him. Word travelled fast. Jack Hoffmann was back in town!

The big man walked along Main and turned down the side street to Mrs O'Casey's rooming-house. The white clapboard building had a pleasant appearance. It was well maintained and as he stepped up on to the stoop, the sweet smell of summer flowers meandered across his senses. Pots of prairie roses and geraniums had been placed either side of the doorway and were set out inside the house in profusion. The gorgeous fragrance met him at the doorway and from an open casement window to his left. The clean, sweet smell was in strong contrast to the dirt and trail dust he had become used to over the past days.

'Well there you are, Mr Hoffmann! It'll be some of my coffee you'll be after, I'll warrant.' The red-haired Irish woman smiled and nodded towards the tray she was holding.

Hoffmann took off his stetson. 'Thank yuh, ma'am.'

She indicated for him to come closer. 'Mister Sourdough Joe Turner has just told me all about you, an' how you used to be sheriff here before me an' my late, dear departed husband joined the town.' She blushed a little. 'Said I could call him Sourdough an' asked if I could provide one of my best downstairs rooms for your good self, so he did. To conduct your business matters from. An' you not having to pay a penny piece in rent for it either! Mister Sourdough said that our Mister Timmings of the Citizens' Committee would pick up the bill when you have finished your work! Sourdough's been up to see him. Isn't that nice?' The plump, middle-aged woman smiled, revealing a row of white teeth which accentuated her ruddy complexion. 'I've shown Miss Bethan an' Mister Sourdough their rooms an' now they're waiting for you in your new office!' She added proudly, 'If you'd like to go in, sir, I'll bring this coffee through for you all.' She indicated to a door on the right of the vestibule.

Sourdough was packing his corncob with

tobacco and talking to Bethan when the door opened. His eyes twinkled with excitement as he saw Hoffmann. 'Howdy, pilgrim. Miss Bethan an' me wuz just a-chewin' the cud over what yuh might have found out. Anythin' interestin'?'

'Yeah. I think I have, Sourdough. What's all this about yuh seeing Jake Timmings – didn't realise yuh was a-knowing of folks in these parts?' Hoffmann threw his hat on top of a coat stand in the corner and looked hard at the oldtimer.

Sourdough stretched himself back into the chair. 'Well, truth is, pilgrim, I don't know many folks in this neck o' the woods. But you wuz a big man around here a few years back an' well, I figured we'd need ta have somewhere ta meet an' then I met this fella who said that he knowed Mister Timmings, an' the door of the fella's office wuz open an'...'

Hoffmann's eyes bored into the old man. ''Spect yuh meant well enough, but check with me first will yuh? Case we go offending folks's sensibilities around here.'

'Yessir!' The old man's face shone with enthusiasm as the gunfighter sat down.

The room was small, but pleasant, with a rectangular walnut table in the middle and

147

six chairs set around it, all smelling of wood polish. To one side, a mahogany bookcase was half full of old books and flowers bedecked the top.

'Thank yuh kindly, ma'am,' he offered as Mrs O'Casey walked up, set the tray down and began serving them. When the door closed behind her a minute later Hoffmann got to his feet and quietly walked across to the door, listened for a moment, then opened it a little and checked outside.

'Is your information that hot?'

Hoffmann returned to his chair. 'Mebbe, mebbe not. But no matter. It's always nice ta know who yuh dealin' with, Sourdough.'

'She is an extremely pleasant lady!' Bethan suddenly glared at Hoffmann and her voice held anger.

'I'm sure she is, Miss Mackenzie. But my pa taught me ta always cut the cards afore yuh play. Now let's get down to business!'

He outlined the meeting with Roy Cooder and how Cooder's deputy, Chas Clayton had seen the soft-shell, Silas Smith riding a big black across the Double D spread and heading towards cattleman Thomas's ranch house. Hoffmann told them of his intention to go and see Thomas first thing the next day. Sourdough could not be sure, but

Thomas's name had a ring to it that was tantalisingly just out of reach. The gunfighter's dark eyes rested on him. 'What do yuh think, oldtimer?'

'Sounds OK.' Sourdough lit his pipe. 'Only way to follow th' spoor is to talk to this Bill Thomas!'

Hoffmann looked at Bethan Mackenzie, inviting comments. In spite of everyone's preoccupation with events, her closeness suddenly overwhelmed his senses. The big man's eyes were drawn to the gentle curve of her shoulders, the black laced, pink blouse under her tasselled shawl and firm breasts that were pressing invitingly, beneath. His gaze lifted to the brightness of her face. A teasing smile was on the edge of her sensuous mouth as she spoke and big blue eyes filled his spirit with a sudden longing.

'You want the opinion of a mere woman, Mister Hoffmann? I am honoured!'

The gunfighter showed no reaction to her provocation and gave a curt reply. 'Yes, ma'am.'

Bethan knew quite clearly what effect she was having on his emotions and felt a short, powerful thrill of pleasure.

'Good Book says, honour yuh mother and father. Figure that goes fer daughters and sons as well.'

Bethan's smile was suddenly replaced by a look of determination, as she rallied her thoughts. 'I am convinced Silas Smith is in league with the devil over this matter. I can offer no proof at the moment, only strong feelings – woman's intuition if you like.' She paused for a moment. 'I have a feeling Smith does have a direct connection with this rancher, Bill Thomas. You intend going over to see him tomorrow and say you will be keeping a look-out for any sign of Silas whilst you're there. I feel the same now goes for my brother; I believe Daniel might well be held captive by these people. Would you agree?'

Hoffmann nodded slowly.

The old man whistled after watching the other two intently. 'Yuh sure as heck don't like this Silas Smith fella, does yer Miss Bethan?'

'No I don't, Sourdough.' She suddenly straightened in the chair. The milk-white features were now flushed with emotion. Bethan brushed black tresses aside and glowered. 'I know by all that's right, that Silas Smith has had a major hand in the abduction of my brother and until somebody shows me different, I'm going to pursue that man to the ends of the earth if necessary, to prove it!' She sat for some moments, a fire-glow of energy lighting her beautiful eyes.

A knock came on the door. Hoffmann walked across and opened it. Mrs O'Casey said something quietly to him and handed in a note. He returned to the chair, waved the note and placed it beside him on the table. 'Before we get on to this, I'll talk some on what I propose to do tomorrow, based on th' information we have gained so far. I'd like your agreement, so we can work together.' His eyes caught Bethan's. 'I'm sure you'll say ifn yuh don't agree with me!'

She made no reply.

'I'll ride over to Thomas's ranch first thing tomorrow and keep a look-out for any sign of our Mister Smith whilst there and, as you suggest Miss Bethan, keep a weather eye open for Daniel.

'Then I'll ride some. Down trails through the mountains an' follow my instinct fer anythin' that has a feel o' spoor about it. I'd like you two to check out any leads you can find in the town. Go see Sheriff Cooder: he's an old friend of mine and will be helpful. Meet yuh all back here in a day or two an' we can chew a spell on what's been found. Yuh all with me on that?'

'Yes, sir. With yer all the way, pilgrim!' Sourdough was swathed in tobacco smoke and enthusiasm, as he nodded intently.

'Bethan?'

She smiled. The brightness had returned to her face. 'Yes. Sounds excellent to me.'

'Well I'm mighty pleased to hear that, ma'am. Now let's turn to this here note.' He took the small piece of dirty, folded paper and pushed it across to Sourdough.

The old man's face dropped a little as he unfolded it. 'Left mah readin' glasses back at the shack. Truth is, pilgrim, I ain't never done too much ciphering an' the like.'

Hoffmann indicated for him to pass the note to Bethan. 'It says I'm to meet someone back o' the livery stables if I want to hear news of President Mackenzie's son!'

'Dang mah ol' breeches!' Sourdough jumped to his feet. 'I'll cover yuh from the back o' the corn chandler's. This could be it, Jack! Let's go git the varmint!'

The bounty hunter stood up and put his hand on the oldtimer's shoulder. 'Got a more important job for yuh, Sourdough. I want yuh to look after Miss Bethan, here. Yuh never known, this could be a sleight of hand; yuh knows what I mean, oldtimer? Get me away an' then make a grab for the girl!' He winked carefully at Bethan. 'Them crittas would have both son an' daughter of the President then!'

'Well dang me! Ain't a thought o' that one, pilgrim. No, sir. But I'll do it fer yuh, Jack. Yers can rely on ol' Sourdough Joe!' His twinkling blue eyes shone with excitement and he turned to Bethan. 'Now you won't be afraid none, will yuh, Miss Bethan? I'll look after yuh real good.'

Bethan gave affirmation as Hoffmann picked up his stetson from the hat stand and slid the note into his pocket. The old man was still talking avidly when Jack Hoffmann walked quietly out of the room.

EIGHT

The solitary range rider stood waiting at the far end of a back alley, which twisted a cluttered route among storage sheds and backs of shops on the main street of Pine Ridge, behind the livery stables. The cowboy was greasy, dirty and thin. Small, urgent eyes moved uneasily and a gleam of sweat shone on his forehead in the bright sunlight. He was about nineteen years of age, with a long, weather-beaten face like teak. He wore a checked rangeman's shirt, leather chaps tied loosely over faded denim pants and scuffed brown riding boots. A revolver was holstered cowboy style, high on his right hip and a flat-crowned, brown hat hung at his back. The stranger's eyes, slitting in the bright, dusty light, were carefully scanning the staggered alleyway either side of him.

It was early evening and not a cloud defaced a bright clear blue sky. The sun was dropping slowly in the west and burned diagonally along the narrow walkway, offering shadows on the dirt path in advance of

155

anyone's approach. To the rangeman's right, the alley was nearly blocked by wooden boxes, discouraging anyone from entering, but leaving a bolt hole should he need it.

Jack Hoffmann walked purposefully down Main and stopped outside the livery stables. He felt an instinctive unease at a scenario which could be a crude, but very effective, set-up to kill him; or equally, a naive attempt at a clandestine meeting, where the arranger had little knowledge of the utterly devious nature of some of his fellow men.

Hoffmann knew that he would have to enter that alley-run, because the possibility of first hand knowledge of Daniel Mackenzie's whereabouts could not be missed. He checked the Peacemaker and then felt the warm reassurance of the smooth-grained, stubby handle of the scattergun, at his left hip. He remembered with sudden, crystal clear perception the years spent as a deputy and the life-lore he learned at the side of one of the best gunfighters he had ever known – Quincy Lane; a one-time killer who had turned lawman and was Pine Ridge's first sheriff.

'To stay alive is the only hard and fast rule, Jack. Live by it. All other bits o' colourin' only come up behind that one and back it. Ifn you're forced inta a corridor, alley-run, or any sort of powerful restriction on ya movement, there is only one way to come out o' the other end alive. An' that is ta let loose the natural animal inside yourself!

'Remember when we wuz in that ghost town out east of Scottsbluff an' had ta move through seven guns, an' only the two on us to do it? Yuh didn't have that ol' scattergun then, an' the firin' pin done broke in ya Peacemaker on ya first squirt at one o' them. What did ya do, boy? I'll tell yuh. You become native to the place – like an Injun. Ya used ya sense o' smell, ya eyes, hearin', body speed, stealth and pulled it all together naturally, like a draw-string pulls around a money bag. The animal inside yuh then came a-sneakin' out – to kill! He's in us all, that critta; when survival calls. Most men an' women folks never even know he exists, or understand what a powerful friend he can be. That beast can come out anywheres, city or country, mountain or mine.

'You broke the neck o' one man with yuh bare hands an' knocked the other two unconscious with the Colt ya took from the first. Mine wuz the easy job. I had the Winchester an' cover to shoot from. Ifn ya didn't realise

157

it then, Jack, realise it now. Yuh wouldn't be here ifn it weren't fer that animal. He saved your life!'

The range rider's head jerked as he heard something in the alley ahead of him. It was the time of evening meals now. Sounds of cooking, domestic disputes, gathering of families and friends drifted on the air. Inconspicuously, from out of those sounds came the quiet, almost indistinguishable footfall of someone walking steadily on the rock hard ground. The pace of the newcomer's approach was even and very deliberate. Suddenly the young cowboy could see a long shadow growing where the alley turned from his sight and he realised the advanced warning that the sun was giving. The shadow stopped moving in an instant, then vanished. Silence.

'Your name Jack Hoffmann?' The cowboy's voice had a slight thinness of fear to it.

The shadow appeared again and a tall man entered the confined passage thirty yards away, his low-crowned stetson shading dark features.

'Said, your name Hoffmann?' Again the thinness in the sound betrayed fear.

'That's mah name.'

The bounty hunter started to walk foward. He was dressed all in black; the rhythmical sound of leather boots on the pathway joined by the quiet tinkling of rowels rotating in his spurs.

The ranger saw the newcomer's features, a big man, tall and dark with eyes that were boring right through him. He also saw the shining leather brass and steel of the man's gun rig. A revolver was at his right hip and what looked like a cut-down scattergun on his left. He came nearer, the animal rhythm having a freezing effect upon the cowboy's sensibilities, like a deer being stalked by a cougar. Suddenly the tall figure was standing right there in front of him, like a brooding premonition of death.

'Yuh got a message fer me? The where-abouts o' someone I needs to meet!' The words were spoken with a cold precise cadence, somewhere between a whisper and a low growl. Hoffmann looked right into the ranger's face, a young and frightened face, as if something had been started that would have been best left undone.

'You're the Jack Hoffmann who's helping the lady from out East?'

The gunfighter nodded slowly. 'That Jack Hoffmann. Whatta ya know, son? Spit it out an' we kin both get ourselves some vittles an' settle fer the evenin'.'

The youngster looked around nervously. 'Name's Tranter, Al Tranter. Got sacked this afternoon for hittin' the foreman at the Double D spread.'

'Bill Thomas's outfit?'

'Yeah. His beeves are still dying. Never got over last winter's famine.'

'Bad all round, so I hears.'

'Yeah. Real bad, Mister Hoffmann. I've lived around beeves all my life. 'S all I knows, but I knows that work as well as any man. And Thomas is as good as done for. He's gonna lay off all his hands in a few days. They don't know yet, but I heard it good.

'Foreman caught me outside, listening at the kitchen door. Pete's OK an' I wish I hadn't hit him now...'

Something instinctive in Hoffmann's heightened senses caused him to pull back as a deafening report exploded from the other side of a shiplap wooden wall. The young cowboy, taken utterly by surprise, was killed instantly by a large calibre slug that passed through his chest and blew lung tissue and heart muscle out against the opposite wall. As Hoffmann drew 'Betsy' and turned in a flash of time, a second shot passed within a inch of his head. The gunfighter ignited the scatter gun as he came in contact with the ground and started to roll across the path. The massive fire-flash blew splintered wood away from the planked wall and hit the assailant centrally with the full devastating force that the big bore gun offered in anger. The man was hurled back against a large lumber post directly behind him and then thrown forward to come crashing out of the tattered, wooden wall. He collapsed halfway out; red gore, entrails and stomach contents spread around the body. The trembling form was lifeless. It continued to heave and kick for a short while, even though the gun-fighter's lightning reactions had blown the assassin to eternity.

Jack Hoffmann's senses returned quickly to the sounds of horses whinnying behind in the livery stables. A dog started barking and the cries of startled people grew quickly. He stood up and reloaded the hot scattergun, then turned among the hubbub of voices to see men peering at him over the piled boxes. The onlookers were torn half-way between blood-lust and fear of being shot themselves.

'Get Sheriff Cooder down here right away.' Hoffmann's words were almost matter-of-fact.

'Who are you?' A freckle-faced youth of about fifteen years, had his mouth open as he stared back in astonishment at the big man.

Voices rose from behind the pile, chastising, threatening. 'That's Jack Hoffmann yuh danged young fool. Go on – do what he says. Skedaddle – quick, now.' The sound of running footsteps vanished up Main as the boxes were moved and the passage cleared. 'We've sent for Doc Levis.'

'No need, they're both dead.'

Townsfolk squeezed themselves into the confined space and when the body was lifted from the shed opening and turned over, a cry of astonishment went up. The whitened features and empty eyes of Sam Harper stared up as his mortal remains were laid out on the bloodied dirt floor. The undertaker would attend only one more funeral in Pine Ridge – his own.

Two names had been on Jack Hoffmann's lips when he had returned to the cow-town, those of Silas Smith and an unknown man called Harper. Now it would seem one was dead already, and a drifting cowboy taken as well. Hoffmann determined there and then to trace the doings of the other man, before deviousness and killing could go any further.

Early the following morning, the one-time sheriff and now professional gunfighter from Dakota Territory set off on a three-hour journey to see rancher Bill Thomas, as he had promised. A short ride set him on the trail that ran from Pine Ridge to Lander. After an hour or so, he turned off and started the climb up on to range-land among draws and gulches spread out in an open ended valley in the Green mountains that Thomas called his own.

Soon Hoffmann was riding across prairie where the buffalo once roamed free and had since been won from the wild, by the guts and sweat of men to feed America's growing population.

As Jack Hoffmann crossed the range, he saw first hand what had been on people's lips for many months – the terrible drought of last winter was still having a bad effect on the land. Either side, as far as he could see, the white bones and rotting carcasses of cattle lay on the plains in profuse abandonment. Odd drifts of tumbleweed crossed the horse's path as he rode in bitter dismay at the sights around him. Man and horse eased their way down to the floor of a draw and ahead a lean, range-hardened bunch of cowboys were driving scraggy beeves. The men were brave and skilful. They rode on low-horned range saddles, turning and running their horses quickly with great dexterity among the herd; hazing cattle out of the draws, gulches and brush thickets energetically. Hoffmann watched with respect. The land began a slow fall through broad miles of Wyoming prairie, scrub and chaparral that hid a few wild steers and Hoffmann could make out the form of habitation in the distance. He approached looking carefully at the buildings, taking everything in, as was his way.

The Double D ranch house was of fair size and solid construction, built from pine logs and under a good slate roof. A habitation of men only was the probability, Hoffmann decided, for little evidence of anything feminine could be seen.

The dwelling was accompanied by sod-roofed barns, a few sheds, the windows being covered with tarpaper, and two corrals. Ash and birch trees formed a windbreak to the house itself and to the far left stood the outline of the long, single-story lumber bunkhouse for the range hands.

As Hoffmann rode Jess down from a spinney where the trail turned right, carrion crows squawked and wheeled overhead, and the yip-yip-yip of cowboys at their work could be heard drifting downwind of the depleted herds. Jess crossed on to an oasis of thick grass in front of the ranch house where the cattle were kept from feeding, deadening the drubbing of her hoof beats on the dry ground. As Hoffmann swung down from the saddle, the front door opened and a middle-aged, thickset man appeared in the doorway.

'I'm taking no more hands on this season, friend, so be on your way!'

'Not lookin' fer work. Lookin' fer Daniel Mackenzie. Yuh heard o' the fella?'

The bounty hunter's blunt approach was deliberate and the man's shock at the words could not be missed.

'Never heard of him. Who's asking?'

'Hoffmann. Jack Hoffmann.'

The man looked astonished for a split second, then regained himself.

Hoffmann continued. ''Spect yuh've heard o' Sam Harper, though! Undertaker over at Pine Ridge.'

The man made to consider for a moment. 'No. Why?'

'He shot dead one o' your hands yesterday. Name o' Tranter.'

'Why'd he do that?'

'The young fella was about to tell me where I could find Dan Mackenzie. Seems Mister Harper didn't like the idea none too much.'

'I don't know anything about this, Mister Hoffmann. What's happened to Harper?'

'He's been laid out in his mortuary. I shot him before he could do any more harm.'

The rancher looked Hoffmann up and down, weighing matters. Then he smiled. 'Guess you'd like to come in for a spell?'

Hoffmann took his hat off. 'Be obliged to yuh, Mister Thomas.'

The rancher stabbed a finger at him. 'Wait there a moment.'

Hoffmann tied Jess to the hitching rail outside and patted the horse. 'Good girl, Jess.'

Bill Thomas returned to the doorway and called the bounty hunter in. The two men walked through to a large sitting-room where the embers of last night's fire simmered in a huge stone fireplace. Above the mantelpiece, hung an ornate mirror and above it two browning horns protruded from a large ox's skull, mounted on the wall. Heavy furniture of quality when new was set out around the room. The stained floor-boards were uncovered and the room had a

166

smell of pinewood and worn leather.

'Set yourself down a spell, Mister Hoff-mann. I had that new deputy from Pine Ridge up here sniffin' about a couple days ago. An' I done told him there ain't no man around here with an eye-patch. Never wuz an' never has been all the time I've been here. Now you seem ta think I've got a fella here by the name o' Daniel...'

'Mackenzie.'

'Yeah. An' I ain't. No offence intended Mister Hoffmann, but why do you folks from Pine Ridge think fellas are livin' up here who ain't?'

'It's a long story.' Hoffmann scanned the rancher and the room for any clue as the man stood in front of his fireplace and lit a cheroot with a spill from the fire ashes. He was in his early fifties with a thick, bull-like neck, still fairly brown hair and a full, silvered mou-stache which drooped over the ends of his mouth. Brown, yellow flecked eyes had guile written into them; his face and manner showed a domineering intelligence that seemed almost to enjoy confrontation.

An employee dressed in sweat-stained clothes and a dirty apron came in with a tray of coffee. Thomas offered the black treacle-like liquid, milk and sugar, with a hard attempt at casual civility. Hoffmann accepted a cup as it was. He worked through his tale of events in simple terms, not allowing Thomas to know too much of their progress. It became very clear as the conversation grew that Thomas was as clever, cunning and worldly as his appearance implied. Jack Hoffmann couldn't draw a thing from him and asked about the cattleman's ranch. He was surprised at the openness of the reply. Bill Thomas was clearly proud of his last five years' work on the Double D and that seemed justifiable.

'Bought a quarter-section and a log cabin from a homesteader family who couldn't make a go of farmin' the land, five years ago. Got some labour over from various parts an' rebuilt the cabin into a ranch house; included a bunkhouse and converted other buildings to get into raising cattle. This quarter-section plot is in a valley between the mountains, as yer can see, an' opens out further on to the public domain prairie where anyone can graze. There wuz no one else on it then, but I knew there soon would be! I pastures my beef cattle here now an' up there on the open prairie, fattening it fer the market over in Rawlins, where they freight it east.

'The last winter was real bad. Some ranchers had their herds wiped out by cold and starvation and were forced out of business.' He grinned and flicked ash in the fireplace. 'I'm a business man, Mister Hoffmann, not a country hick. I wasn't raised around these parts, an' cattle is just a means o' earnin' a living to me. I'll climb back up again in the future.'

That part Hoffmann had respect for and he acknowledged the fact to the rancher. As he was shown out, the two men passed a small cloakroom and the bounty hunter noticed a good quality top coat among the range garb hanging there. It was of similar colour and appearance to the coat Hoffmann remembered lying next to Silas Smith at the meeting in Indian Wells. The likelihood of any cowboy owning or even needing such refined city wear was so remote that the chances of a city slicker being there, either staying for a few days, or just plain visiting, seemed to him to be a very good possibility. Maybe Bethan Mackenzie's womanly instincts were right after all!

Hoffmann left the ranch house and rode along a route leading down to the main trail, which headed west. When out of sight, he back tracked and settled down in a spinney,

169

concealing himself from sight and obtaining clear views back to the ranch house, some five hundred yards away. He took out a pair of field glasses from the saddlebag and sat down to wait, rolling himself a cigarette. After half an hour had passed uneventfully, a figure emerged and rode down the quarter-section at a good gallop. The rider was travelling along the same trail that led past the spinney. Hoffmann looked through the field glasses and was astonished at the sight that met his eyes.

The horseman, riding skilfully and hard, was the soft-shell easterner, Silas Smith! His eye-patch and facial discolouration could be seen clearly, before the gunfighter lost sight of him as he vanished into a draw. A few minutes later, Jack Hoffmann swung up into the saddle and headed Jess down through the cover of mesquite and oaks in the direction of Smith's hurried flight. He followed without incident until reaching the trail west. Then searching around, he picked up the galloping horse's fresh hoof prints that were heading towards a small town Hoffmann knew to be Selcott Acre.

So Smith had deliberately lied to everyone. Bethan's womanly intuition was right after all. Silas Smith and the ranch owner were

now clearly in cahoots over some deviousness and when the facts were lined up, the
smell from it was bad enough to stun a
polecat!

Eleven o'clock the following morning, Jack
Hoffmann, Bethan and Sourdough gathered
for a second meeting, this time with Sheriff
Roy Cooder in the law-office down on Main.
Jack explained all that he had found, including the culmination of Silas Smith's
hurried journey, which ended at Selcott
Acre. He then told them about seeing the
easterner there, drinking in a saloon with a
gunfighter Hoffmann knew well as China
Kid Ory. Hoffmann had once worked briefly
with Kid Ory and was very much aware and
respectful of his deadly guns. The two men
sitting in the saloon had been in deep conversation, which could have been legitimate
business in connection with finding Daniel,
except that Smith was now known to have
stayed secretly with Bill Thomas, a man
under much suspicion.

'Well, what do yuh think, Roy?'

Sheriff Cooder nodded slowly and his
deep, growling voice oozed across the
wooden room, holding the gathering like a
velvet clad hand. 'Well I'll tell yer, Jack, Bill

Thomas's story is a mite short o' the full truth. He ain't fully coloured the picture.'

'No?'

'No. It's true that five years ago he did buy out a homesteader called Russell. But there were rumours suggestin' the Russell family were strongly pressurised to accept Thomas's offer. Nothin' proven yer understand, but his drinking water got bad an' they wuz all ill for weeks. Saddlebums would ride through when they had no call to an' they'd be likkered up an' start shootin' hell outa the livestock ta scare 'em up. Horses ruined the kitchen crops by ridin' all over an' such like. Russell had two fires in his barns for no account. One in the middle o' winter with snow everywheres!'

'What happened to the family?'

'Steve Russell was ill for some time an' died o' dysentery on the road to Medicine Bow. Nice fella. Knew him well enough. Good countryman an' father to his three kids. Don't know what happened to his family exactly. Heard they moved on east.'

'I can add a little to this.' Bethan's clear feminine voice contrasted to the sheriff's tones and her eyes were bright. 'My father says that things are quickly changing and the time is now coming for homesteaders and barbed wire. The open ranges with cattle free to roam across unoccupied public prairie land is now as good as dead. It'll be privately owned ranches covering thousands of acres from now on. Could this be the last nail in Bill Thomas's coffin and a good reason for him to become embroiled in kidnapping?' She looked at Jack Hoffmann. 'What do you think, Mister Hoffmann?'

'I guess yuh could be right. I ain't a farmer, rancher or no politician. But I figure if Thomas is the kidnapper o' yuh brother, the motive for him choosing such a way of obtaining money, must surely be because his days are now numbered.

'Funny thing is, when I was talkin' to him, there was somethin' in his voice, the way he spoke as if I'd heard him before.' Hoffmann rubbed his chin. 'Yuh know, like you'd recognise kinfolks yuh ain't never met before. He ain't no kin o' mine, but I seem to have met someone with a voice just like his, recent like.' He turned to Cooder. 'Are any local folks related to him?'

The sheriff shook his head. 'Not that I know of. Nope, he ain't from around these parts.'

They both looked at Bethan Mackenzie, who was smiling broadly. 'I think I might know who Bill Thomas's brother is!' She looked at the others triumphant.

'When I was a little girl father asked Silas Smith to look after me sometimes, when mother and he were on business. Smith would be there tagging along to meet all the right people and father would send us off to the park or somewhere.' She laughed. 'Even as a child I knew he was well out of his league trundling an eight-year-old girl around and having to buy her candy. I used to play him up, giving out all sorts of stories of woe.' She smiled. A kindly, unexpected smile. 'Even someone as selfish and ruthless as he is, sometimes has a little bit of humanity somewhere that he is trying to suppress. He used to pacify me with stories, some fairy-tales, others about himself before the war with the South. His father died when he was very young and the mother married again. From this marriage came a second son – Silas's half-brother. I can't remember the boy's name, but I know they were great friends in his younger days. When they grew up, the brother moved out West somewhere to be with his father's people.'

'What are yuh saying, ma'am?' Roy Cooder's gruff voice held astonishment.

'I'm saying, Mister Cooder, that I will go

down to the telegraph office now and ask the head of my father's senate committee to send me the name of Silas Smith's half-brother.'

Sourdough's eyes lit up. 'Yer gonna telegraph Washington DC? They'll never believe ya. They'll think ya a crank, beggin' yuh pardon an' all. How'll they know it's you?'

'Oh they will know it's me all right, Sourdough.' She stood up. 'The rancher you all know as Bill Thomas, is Silas Smith's secret half-brother, and I am going to prove it!' Bethan strode out of the room leaving the three men looking at each other in stunned silence.

NINE

Two hours after the meeting in Sheriff Cooder's law-office, Jack Hoffmann was settled outside on the veranda of Mrs O'Casey's rooming-house with a good meal inside of him. Sourdough had gone off to do some work for Jake Timmings and Bethan was upstairs in her room after visiting the telegraph office. The gunfighter sat on the veranda deep in thought, weighing the problems and possibilities that lay ahead. His feet were up on the rail and his hat tipped down over his eyes, when a slow, familiar voice broke the silence.

'Howdy.'

The big man pushed up his stetson and looked up to see Roy Cooder's deputy, Chas Clayton, standing beside the veranda.

'Sorry I missed yuh meetin' earlier on, Jack. There wuz a little bother that had some need o' sorting down at the Cattleman's Bank – teller an' a customer didn't see eye to eye. An' someone had ta show 'em hows to git along a little better. Been a-talkin' ta Roy

177

an' he says it looks like China Kid Ory could be around these parts. Yuh figure?'

'Yeah. I figure, Chas. Gonna wait here an' chew on things a while. Work on the best way ta tackle Thomas, but easy – make sure I wins the game. An' while I chew the cud, serves a purpose too. Ready for the Kid ifn he comes; an' ifn he don't, I'm a-ready anyways.'

The deputy nodded, his dour face casual. 'An' if he comes inta town fer yuh, Roy an' me have got a dooty ta keep the peace. Sure as hell we don't want ta get in between you two! Figure it'll be best all round ifn you accept our guns, Jack.'

Hoffmann looked suddenly grim. 'No back-up, Chas – tell Roy that. I don't want too many folks a-gettin' caught up. I know the Kid an' I'll handle him myself.'

'T'ain't no one this side o' Washington could give Roy Cooder a message liken that, in his own town. He jest might take offence.' The Texan's slow drawled answer was blunt.

Hoffmann settled himself in the wicker chair. 'Meant no offence, an' I reckon Roy wouldn't take any by it.' He looked hard into the eyes of Clayton. 'I don't want no unnecessary killin', Chas – that means no back-ups. Wanta play this one my way. OK?'

The deputy looked at Hoffmann for some

time and then nodded. 'Figure yuh knows the score by now. But remember, ifn yuh change yuh mind, Jack, you've got some good friends in this here town. Just remember that, will yuh?'

The big man eased his feet across the rail. 'Thanks. I'll remember.'

Clayton touched the rim of his stetson and walked slowly down to Main. He turned on to the boardwalk and as Hoffmann resumed his repose, the slim Texan disappeared among townsfolk busy about their business.

At that moment, under the wind-pump at the town's entrance, a dusty rider dismounted and looked down Main. He removed a wide-brimmed stetson hat, then a dirt spattered bandanna from around his neck, dipping it into the catchment tank to wipe his face with the cooling water. The lathered horse beside him drank thirstily from an iron-bound wooden bucket he had filled. The animal looked hard used. It was a solid looking, big steeldust gelding, wearing a fancy saddle rig that had seen many miles of wear. The man was fresh and alert by contrast, as if the journey to Pine Ridge had been a time of ease for him and now he had woken from half-slumber. He took out a gold pocket watch and noted the time of almost half past one.

The stranger was in his late thirties and the oriental blood coursing his veins revealed itself clearly in his appearance. He had close-cropped silver-grey hair, which seemed to accentuate the high cheek-boned, fleshy features of a hard, worldly face. His slanted eyes were very bright, and moved all the time: restless, searching, checking, waiting. He was dressed in riding boots, buckskin pants and wore a brown leather waistcoat over a white sleeved shirt. Two massive .54 Colts holstered on his polished gun belt, were held by leather thongs over the hammers.

The Chinaman put on his stetson and called out to a red-haired youth sitting on the stoop of the freight office. 'Hey you boy, come over here!'

Minutes later Hoffmann heard a faint commotion up on Main. People were talking excitedly and he roused from his reverie. In the distance a young voice spoke his name. 'He's come fer Mister Hoffmann. There's gonna be a gunfight. China Kid Ory's come fer Jack Hoffmann!' Then the sound of running feet on the boardwalk. Suddenly the figure of a red-haired boy shot out of the gap in front of the Golden Garter saloon and turned down the side road, sprinting the final distance to Hoffmann, who was now standing by the veranda rail. The lad was breathing heavily and fought to get his breath.

'There's a Chinese-looking man called Kid Ory at the beginning of town,' the lad panted. 'Gave me a quarter to come and tell you so, and to say he wants to talk to yer, Mister Hoffmann. Says he wants ta talk to yer now!' The lad grinned between breaths. 'I'll go back an' tell him yourn a-coming fer another quarter!'

The bounty hunter paused. 'He'll wait, son.'

The youngster stared back waiting for more and when nothing was forthcoming, he turned on his heels and ran back down the street, his long red hair bouncing with his strides.

'Mister Hoffmann?'

Jack turned to see a dusty range-worn man standing about thirty yards up the street on the other side. He was dressed in cowboy garb and walked over.

'Sorry ta catch yer ill-timed, like this. Name's Pete Steadman, ex-foreman of the Double D. Been a-lookin' all over for yer.

Thomas has laid every one of his hands off, including me. I was the last to go – left this morning.'

Hoffmann was checking the Colt. 'What can I do fer yuh, Mister Steadman?'

'Nothing fer me. It's just that the town's full o' talk about you a workin' fer the President.'

The gunfighter smiled. 'Not directly, Mister Steadman.'

'No. But yer a-lookin' fer his son ain't yer? That's yer contract?'

Hoffmann nodded. 'It's that widely known?'

'Yeah. It would seem so. Folks have been a-talkin'. You were up at the Double D spread yesterday. So yer know the place a bit. Well, he's got someone held up out the back there. No one knows about it, but I overheard a few weeks ago and wuz sworn to secrecy. They've paid me short on mah money, so's I've got no loyalty now. Don't know who the fella is. They just a-call him the boy. He's in a small, secure cabin about sixty yards out the back o' the ranch house, in some tree cover. I'm a-tellin' yer 'cos o' what yer a-doing fer the President an' 'cos they're a-movin' out tonight, takin' every-thing they kin carry on horse an' in buck.'

The big man leaned on the veranda.

'Mighty obliged ta yuh, mister. Any idea where they're heading?'

'No, sir.'

'He got any guns up there?'

'Reckon so. Thomas has linked up with four no-account gunslicks over the last few weeks – mean crittas. He calls 'em enforcers and they live in the ranch house.'

Hoffmann spun the Colt's chamber twice and dropped the six-gun back in its holster. 'Got some business awaitin' on me now as yuh probably knows, but if I sees yuh in the saloon any time I'll buy yuh a snort.' He swung his long legs over the rail and walked off down on to Main, preparing quickly for what was to come. Pete Steadman stared after him for some moments and then walked off in the direction of the stockyards.

Hoffmann passed an empty shop and then the dry-goods store as he strode along the creaking boardwalk. People watched him go. The firm tread of a big man, with spurs jingling; subtle, yet unmistakable animal movement in his long gait, the eyes of townsfolk following the broad, straight back as he went striding by. The cow-town's familiar streets and the voices of old acquaintances brought bad times back to Hoffmann. Times when he had to kill well. He let the moments fill his heightened senses – conditioning himself for what was to come.

Killer: the seventeen-year-old range hand woke to see eyes shining in the moonlight, no more than a foot from his face. The smell of whiskey, the warm breath and then a hand sliding inside his bed roll. Slimy, cold, dirty and strong; the glint of the big Bowie knife near to his eye. 'I wants yer, sonny.' The scramble for the old Dragoon Colt under his pillow – bought last week with his first pay. A quick searing light and the shock of detonation. The scream. The heat, smoke, the dirt. Blood, on him, his clothes, the bed roll. Loud voices, now. Death. The first.

Pine Ridge seemed to have slowed. People were coming out of shops, standing, watching, waiting. He touched casual fingers to the low brim of his black stetson, acknowledging respectful greetings, words of encouragement.
  'Howdy ma'am.'
  'Nice ta see yuh again.'
He passed the assay office.
  'Good ta see yer back in town, Mister Hoffmann.'

'Thank yuh, Luke.'

Some men turned away, afraid.

Killer: a man of twenty, twenty-two. Blond hair, lean-handsome, sunburned, and mean as a diamond-back, with cold blue, mean eyes and the fleshy pale lips of a sensuous womaniser. Pretty Boy Clancy, suddenly wide-eyed, with a pain-wracked face, turning, shocked and spinning downwards towards his death. The young sheriff turned away, feeling heat rising from the Peacemaker in his hand.

'We're all with yuh, Mister Hoffmann. Good luck!' It was the sturdy figure of Stan Keating, head of the Citizens' Committee and manager of the stockyard. A man Hoffmann had not seen for five years. Keating stood back, nodding respectfully.

'Obliged.' Hoffmann was at the harness-maker's now. He strode on past the gun-smith's and Silver Spur saloon.

Killer: Jagger was here somewhere. Mean and fanatical. The heat of the sun burning skin like a cooking fire, even though a wind was up. It was a dry, hot wind. The shirt stuck to his back. Tumbleweed rolled and bounced across the dirt road of the ghost town and the banging shutters on the rotting hotel were beginning to spook him. Suddenly Jagger was there, in front, walking like a malevolent apparition through the rising dust towards him.

'You sonofabitch. I'm a gonna blow your goddamn head off...' The crazy man's hand moved in a sudden instant flash of speed, the hammer was fanned to flame and the sheriff of Pine Ridge felt the kiss of hot death singe him twice as he rolled across the road, returning lead in quick successions of noise and brightness, whilst squirming for survival in twisting kicks and rolls among the dust. It took only one: the one that entered the centre of Jagger's chest and blew out splintered bone, gore and mucus from his back. A long spray of splattering wetness laid down on the hot desert roadway. Then silence. And the shutters banged.

Hoffmann crossed Main and walked past the lumberyard. He could see the wind-pump at the town's entrance now, turning high up and heard the faint, distant screech of dry bearings with the passage of the sails. A young girl was there in front of him, no more than seventeen years of age. She had blonde hair and beautiful, large blue eyes. A man came out of a doorway beside her. The gunfighter could see instantly that he was her father and a friend from the lost years of his past.

'Jack. Kate would like to give you something for good luck.'

The girl smiled. 'For you and the President's son.' She tiptoed up and kissed him on his cheek. Then pinned a sprig of heather on to his leather waistcoat. Before Hoffmann could speak, she turned and merged with the crowd on the boardwalk. The man smiled, raised his hand, then followed her.

Jack Hoffmann a man from that small elite, whose legend had been fashioned in his own lifetime. If he was aware of fear, then he offered no sign of it to the world. None whatsoever. Neither grief, anger nor joy was there, among his controlled, calm, calculating features, or in the hypnotic coolness of his eyes. Life and death had taught Jack Hoffmann iron control and the gunfighter knew that he owed his life, such as it was, to the talent.

'Good day, Mister Hoffmann. The Lord preserve you.'

'Thank yuh.' He tipped his hat towards old man Tucker and strode on, the drub of boots on the dirt of Main and the slowly turning sails of the wind-pump now the only sounds to be heard. At the hotel, Hoffmann stopped. Several horses were hitched at the rail and a little further along Main two wagons were at the Wells Fargo freight office in the process of being unloaded. Such was the clamour and excitement that had spread like wild-fire through the town, wagon drivers and even the office clerk had stopped work and were outside, waiting. The town was waiting.

Killer: Mary Jane looked at him sweetly. He knew what was coming as sure as he knew her expression was about to change. 'He's out there somewhere, my love. Maybe not full grown yet, or maybe a man already. He's out there waiting for you. The man who's that little bit quicker, that little bit sneakier than the others, the one who is going to kill you!' He remembered her tears and how he hated to see a woman cry – especially her, Mary Jane. 'You're famous now, my darling. Your guns are known far beyond Pine Ridge. Getting more famous as the days go on. Give it up Jack Hoffmann while you still can. I'll not be a sheriff's widow – even for you, the man I love most in all this world.'

Then he appeared. China Kid Ory. Stepping out quietly from behind the wind-pump gantry; his brown waistcoat flapping in the gentle breeze and the white of his shirt sleeves standing out in the bright sunlight. Silence reigned between them for long seconds.

'Howdy, Kid. Yuh workin' fer Thomas and Silas Smith now?' His voice was firm, deep.

The gunman paused, nodded. 'You're well informed.'

'And if yuh kill me, they'll make yuh rich, eh?'

'Like I say, Jack, you're well informed.'

The wide-brimmed stetson was shading Kid Ory's face but Jack saw the hard, oriental eyes burning at him. Thongs were off the big Colts and Ory's practiced hands were near them. The brown leather waistcoat continued flapping lazily, flashing a gold line of lights momentarily from his watch chain. 'Remember Shilo Ridge? And what yer learned – the hard way?'

'Sure I do. I remember all. I owes yer, an' I don't want to kill yuh!'

Ory laughed. A harsh bitter laugh.

Hoffmann's eyes hardened. 'You're forgettin' yer own gun-lore!'

The man looked at him, questioning.

'Distract an' then kill. That's what yuh used to say. An' when yer threw yuh head back just then, I could have taken it off yer shoulders.'

Ory stared. Suddenly a cold pain filled him, like a knife blade in his stomach, a feeling he had not known in many years.

The big man paused, his dark eyes locked on the Chinaman. 'An' yuh knows it's true, Kid.'

Then Hoffmann saw clearly that which he looked for in all adversaries. A flicker of movement in the eye betraying fear!

Ory shifted position. 'Heard yer got a rep now Jack. Seems it's well deserved. So you remember, eh? Then you'll remember the Karma Teachings of Chang. I remember you laughing. The only man I ever knew who laughed at Lord Chang. And you only a boy too. You're full-grown man now, Jack. Are yer still laughing?'

Hoffmann eased himself gently, letting his body sense his surroundings and slowly flexed his hands, so every sinew in him was ready for that exploding burst of energy he would soon need to kill once more. Perhaps to survive for another time.

'Learned a lot in those years. An' one thing I've learned is never to underestimate the

190

opposition.' He smiled. 'I don't believe in the teachings of Chang, only speed an' luck.' The bounty hunter paused, as the wind blew oven-dry dust across the road between them. 'And now yuh luck's run out, Kid!'

Hoffmann had guessed they were both evenly matched. But Ory was older and now significantly less able in body movements. He knew that if the gunman had any sense he would stay still, concentrating everything into bringing those two huge calibre .54 Colts to bear on him. But the kick from such massive six-guns could marginalise accuracy – and that's what Hoffmann hoped would give him the edge. The pump's screech rose on the wind and suddenly Kid Ory went for both his guns in a blinding instant of time.

The ex-sheriff of Pine Ridge threw himself towards the gantry on his right, his .45 Colt clearing leather in the twinkling of an eye as instant tongues of flame spat from three barrels in unison. Hoffmann rolled across the dirt road and fanned the hammer among burning lead, flame and prairie dust. He saw the Chinaman move with astonishing speed, firing the big Colts a hair's-breadth off the killing line to his foe. Hoffmann felt the hot lead kiss his cheek and body and in the same instant watched one bloody eruption burst across Ory's throat, the other from the left side of his chest. The Chinaman yelled and turned from the massive impact of Hoffmann's .45s, revealing a crimson mass issuing through a ragged hole in his waistcoat. The man almost fell, then regained his stature. He started to master himself and turned back towards his opponent. Hoffmann was full of incredulity. He remained prone on the ground, the six-shooter cocked and aimed towards his adversary.

'If a man has any chance at all to come back at you – shoot!' That was just plain good horse sense. And against every rule he had ever lived by, Jack Hoffmann waited. He had to. To see if...

Kid Ory's bloodied figure stood erect, about twenty-five yards away from Hoffmann. Slowly, an iron will overcame pain and disfigurement with an eerie finality. The Chinaman's stare bored into Hoffmann once more and suddenly he started to walk forward again, both Colts held up in front, the huge barrels pointing towards Jack Hoffmann like cannon mouths out of a crazy dream. Twenty yards. The wind picked up again and blew the wide-brimmed hat away. Ory was smiling. Each footfall threw up small sprays of dust as he walked, his close cropped grey hair now streaked with red. Hoffmann watched a cascade of bright blood and mucus pour out of the man's mouth and down on to his gore spattered chest. Fifteen yards. The eyes were bright, hate-filled, full of Lord Chang. Ten yards. Hoffmann squeezed the trigger slowly as Ory continued walking. Five yards. Dust drifting away sluggishly on the wind. The Chinaman stopped. He stood there, just as Lord Chang had promised him, right in front of his enemy, ready to watch his foe in the finality of death. Hoffmann held back on the trigger pressure, astonished at the reality of what he was seeing. Suddenly, bright eyes were glazed and then, like some old tower of corrupt and ancient history, China Kid Ory slowly toppled over and fell to the ground. Faded eyes rolled upwards. The gunman was dead before he had hit the ground.

Cheers, yells and whoops of exhilaration brought Jack Hoffmann to his feet. He turned to see townsfolk streaming towards him across the open square entrance to Main. Quickly he was surrounded by smiling faces, arms were patting him and girls kissed his cheek. Kid Ory was one thing but this had to be too much for any man! He thanked people, acknowledged warm good wishes and slowly extracted himself to walk firmly back down Main and into town.

'Thank yuh, ma'am.'

'Howdy, there.'

'Yeah, I'm fine thank yuh.'

He walked down past the Wells Fargo office, hotel, corral, livery, builder's yard, farrier and blacksmith. Next to the barber's shop was the telegraph office and outside stood a wiry middle-aged man with grey hair, wearing a green eyeshade.

'Afternoon, Mister Hoffmann! Glad you're OK.'

'Afternoon, Bart.'

The man's eyes were glowing with pleasure. 'Got a reply for Miss Bethan from Washington DC!'

'Yuh want me to take it along to her?'

'Well, I'm s'posed to give it direct to the person who's named on the telegraph form – seeing as it's you though...' He handed the folded sheet to Hoffmann, acknowledged with an index finger to his eyeshade and returned to the equipment on which a small bell had started to ring in the office.

Hoffmann strode on down the boardwalks and opened the sheet.

The flowery, but clear handwritten message was all that Bethan Mackenzie could have hoped for.

Strictly confidential for Miss Bethan M. Mackenzie only. Silas Herbert Smith: President Mackenzie's Aide-de-Camp. The above named person has only one known living relative, a half-brother by the name of William C. Thomas. Last known address: Rushville, Nebraska. Best wishes and God speed Joshua L. Kennedy CSC.

He refolded the form and put it in his waistcoat pocket. Mrs O'Casey was coming out of the front door of the rooming-house when Hoffmann stepped up onto the stoop. She was almost in tears.

'Oh, Mister Hoffmann. I'm so pleased to see you all right. Thank God you've been spared. They've taken her. Two men. Thugs on horses. They brought a third animal, put her on it and tied the poor girl to the saddle whilst everybody was away up the other end of town. They rode off with her about ten minutes ago. Mister Sourdough tried to stop them an' they hit him on the head.'

At that, the door opened and Sourdough stood there, rubbing the back of his scalp.

'Howdy, pilgrim. They've got Miss Bethan.

We've got to git after them!'

'Yuh OK, oldtimer?'

'Sure, sure. I've taken a lot worse 'n that an' I'm still up 'n fighting.'

Hoffmann looked at the cut and it didn't look too bad. He turned to Mrs O'Casey. 'I think he'll be OK if he takes it easy. How are you, ma'am? Did they upset any of yer other guests?'

She shook her head. 'They were all out.'

'I've got to get on the trail o' these people as soon as possible. But I wants to discuss things with Sourdough first. Ten minutes one way or the other ain't a-gonna affect the outcome none. Would yuh be kind enough to bring us some o' your coffee through, please ma'am?'

She smiled and agreed as the two men walked into the office.

''Twas Thomas's lot all right, Jack. Overheard them talkin'. They thought I wuz out cold! Crittas have taken her up to the Double D ranch house.'

Hoffmann nodded and indicated for him to sit down. 'OK. Yuh mentioned on the wagon trip from Oaksville that yuh've got a buffalo gun. Yuh any good with it at long range – an' I don't want yer joshin' me none – folks' lives are at stake here, oldtimer?'

Sourdough looked him in the eye. 'What range yuh talkin'?'

'Five to six hundred yards.'

He nodded. 'Yes, sir. I kin knock a man off a horse as clean as whistling at that range.'

'Yuh've done buffalo huntin' up in Montana, so yuh told me – but a man's a lot smaller target.'

'Yes, sir. But I kin do it.'

'How can yuh be so sure?'

'Cemetery hill, Gettysburg, July '63.'

'Yuh were in the army?'

'No, sir. Scouted for Reynold's First Corps, for a bit.'

'Respect that, Sourdough. But I'm a-wonderin' if I'm askin' a mite too much o' yuh. Gettysburg was a long while ago. An' you havin' ta wear glasses now.'

The old man looked surprised.

'I know yuh only put them on for readin' – fact is I've never seen yuh wearin' them, but...'

'Ah. I sees what yer a-drivin' at, pilgrim. Allow an old fella some pride will yuh? I never wuz much at cipherin' an' readin', so's I...'

Hoffmann interrupted. 'OK, I gets yuh drift. There's a lot at stake here, yuh knows what I'm gettin' at?'

Sourdough nodded. 'Sure. I understands, pilgrim. Yer gets a lot o' charlatans around these days don't yuh?' His blue eyes twinkled. 'What's the plan?'

'Yuh know a spinney on the trail up through Thomas's land, where it turns right about five hundred yards in front of the ranch house?'

Sourdough thought for a moment. 'Yeah. Reckon I knows it. Why?'

'Get that ol' buffalo gun oiled up an' in best order, together with a hog's head o' good ammunition, anything connected ta make yourn shootin' better an' some vittles to keep yuh going for a day or two. Yuh got any powerful field glasses?'

'No, sir.'

'Can yuh get some?'

'Sure. What's the score Jack? What yuh want me to do?'

'We're gonna take Smith, Thomas an' his four strong-arm boys by force.'

'What? Jest the two on us?'

'An' a six-stick bundle o' dynamite. I want yuh to go an' see Jethro Swan at the gun-smith's. He's got some crates in new. Yuh wants new. Yuh understand me, Sour-dough?'

''Course I do. Don't worry none. Yer can

rely on old Sourdough Joe! What time we meet up an' where? In the spinney?'

'Yeah.' Hoffmann took out a pocket watch for his waistcoat. 'Say six o'clock this evening. You got a watch?'

'Sure thing, pilgrim!' Sourdough produced a small, battered, silver bezel chronometer from his pocket and tapped it loudly on the table. 'Good an' accurate as the day it wuz made!'

Mrs O'Casey arrived with coffee and vanished quickly and as quietly as she had come. Hoffmann downed a cupful of the hot liquid and picked up his hat. 'See yuh at six sharp up in that spinney. Don't let anyone know where yuh's a-going. An' no one see yuh enter. OK?'

Sourdough's blue gimlet eyes twinkled back at him. 'Don't yer worry none. I'll be there, pilgrim!'

As the gunfighter pulled the door shut, he heard the old man give a quiet little whoop of excitement. After a second or two of reflection, Hoffmann steeled himself to his decision: this must be the right one, given the short time available – the old man's aim might now have weakened after all those years, but he should still give a reasonable account of himself. That was the gamble and a mighty big one – for the half-crazy plan he was willing to try rested entirely upon a rifleman up in that spinney!

TEN

The trail west of Pine Ridge ran for about two miles between rolling, pine-belted hills and then joined the stage route from Rawlins to Lander. The two-mile stretch reminded Hoffmann of the Black Hills. It was in those hills, at twenty-one years of age, he had panned for gold and nearly lost his scalp to a stealthful Indian brave. The Indian turned out to be a relative of the great Sioux Chief and war leader, Crazy Horse; the man of honour whom white men feared greatly and the Indians called Tashunka Witko. The young brave had befriended Hoffmann and through this friendship which lasted some months, he learned a great deal about tracking both animals and men.

After turning on to the stage trail, Hoffmann followed it north and then broke off east, climbing Jess up towards the prairie and mountains where Thomas's two gunmen had taken the kidnapped girl. He dismounted in places and followed the fresh trail of the three horses without difficulty, guessing that his fast passage had closed the gap between them by a significant margin.

Soon he entered a winding, high wall canyon and a few minutes later a light drizzle started. Jack Hoffmann felt sure his quarry must be ahead in the warren of boulders and scree and set Jess on a fast pace. After some minutes he turned off and made a steep ascent up a firm animal track, urging the still willing horse onwards among boulder grass and scrub bushes. It was a route he had made note of yesterday, when riding over to see Thomas at his ranch. The difficult climb was fairly dangerous, but had the advantage of significantly closing the distance between him and the two gunmen. Even more, at the top, it would furnish him with a worthwhile, but limited, gun sweep over the bottom of the canyon near to the exit, after which the ravine floor opened out into the valley where Thomas's quarter-section was situated. Hoffmann knew the advantage he would have if only he could position himself in time.

As he climbed, stands of timber appeared. He wound his way through the clumps of spruce, birch and mesquite, carefully watching the route ahead. The canyon below was a dark, desolate place and as the rider climbed higher he listened carefully from the quiet, rocking back of the horse for any evidence of his quarry, but to no avail. The light rain stopped, leaving behind a strong aroma from the trees and of rain-stirred juniper and mountain grasses higher up. The warm air was evaporating water from the soil almost as fast as it had fallen. He rode on, making good time, for Jess was a strong, sure-footed animal. They were shortening the distance to the canyon exit minute by minute, by taking this far more direct route on the rocky, steeply inclined trackway. He kept in the cover of what trees and rocks were to be found in case his movements were spotted. Nothing untoward occurred at all and Hoffmann was beginning to think that maybe he had misjudged when, below, a flash of light at about a thousand yards distance caused him to rein Jess to a halt.

The gunfighter dismounted, tied the horse's reins to a small silver birch tree and took a pair of field glasses out of the saddle boot, checking the sun's position first of all, so that the polished lenses would not give his position away. He lay prone on the ground and flicked the knurled centre wheel around to focus. The magnified image of two horsemen, one ahead and the other behind a woman rider on a piebald horse, her hands tied to the saddle horn, leapt up at him in instant array. Bethan! She looked frightened and wary.

The party would be out of sight soon behind a rocky bluff and Hoffmann knew he had about ten minutes to gain the high ground, where his gun sweep could take place. He mounted the horse and gently urged her on. A short time saw him at the small plateau. The gunfighter tied Jess to some bushes and took his much prized '73 Winchester from the saddle holster. The plateau was all that he had hoped for, offering clear views of the narrow trail far below on the canyon floor at about three hundred yards distance from where he stood. A twisting passage through the rocks then disappeared afterwards to the unseen prairie beyond. The gun sweep almost gave him a fairground shooting gallery scenario, insomuch as once Thomas's hirelings had appeared, they would be in vision for about twenty seconds, before disappearing behind the cliff face. Hoffmann knew he would only have time for two shots and that they would both have to count!

He lay on the ground and took aim; staring at the bluff entrance and carefully swinging the octagonal barrel of the Winchester left along the trail, until the gun sight reached the cliff face. Hoffmann repeated the movements, time and time again to get it into his bones. He levered a round into the chamber, took his hat off to reduce the possibility of being spotted and lay down again. Thoughts of Quincy Lane returned to his mind once more. Perhaps it was returning to Pine Ridge, but as he waited, the old sheriff's words came to him vividly:

'Clear yer head o' anythin' other than killin' well. To do that, boy, yer gotta be sure in yer own mind that what yer about ta do is as right as ever destroyin' a man can be. Are yer really prepared to kill him? Remember, killin' someone totally unprepared, is bushwhackin'. An' that's about the meanest thing one man can do to another! You decide Jack, 'cos you gotta sleep nights, an' the time will come, sure as hell is hot, when a man's gonna do somethin' that leaves yuh little choice. Be sure as if it wuz your own life on the line – because in the long run, boy, it probably is!'

Suddenly the first horseman appeared. He wore a black flat-brimmed Mexican-style hat, a black waistcoat, dusty denims and was totally unaware of his plight.

'I'm sure, ol' fella. Yeah, I'm sure an' ready now!'

Hoffmann took aim and kept the gun sight hovering on the man's chest as he slowly rode along the trail. Bethan appeared behind and then the second gunman, bringing up the rear.

Hoffmann waited and then slowly started to squeeze the trigger as the group neared the greatest distance from cover. The report echoed from wall to wall around the canyon as the first rider was thrown from his horse by the impact of the slug passing through his rib-cage and heart. Hoffmann could see Bethan's horse start to rear up as he quickly levered a second shell into the chamber. He swung the carbine past her and took aim at the other gunman, who was now turning and making a run for cover. The heavily built man would be prone for about seven seconds, before reaching safety. Jack Hoffmann's eyes were cool and deadly cold as he brought the gun to bear on the frightened horseman riding back down the trail at full gallop. He squeezed the trigger slowly, following with practised precision and blew the man away with the clinical coldness of an abattoir death. Hoffmann felt no real regret for the action and only a mild satisfaction at his success. The bullet cut through the back of the gunman's head in bloody finality, only three yards away from the cover he was so desperately seeking.

It was done. Hoffmann stood up and shouted down encouraging words to Bethan. He could see her calming the spooked horse with some effect. He hoped she could hear him at that distance and mounted Jess. The big roan mare seemed to sense the urgency and Hoffmann let the horse have its head all the way down. When they reached the floor of the ravine, Bethan's animal was calm and she sat upon its back, white as the death around her.

'You murdering bastard. You've killed two men and it could have been me as well!' Her eyes burned at him with a frightened anger he had never seen before in a woman.

'Yuh not in Washington now, Miss Mackenzie. And I'm in no mood ta take yourn mouth. So shut it!' He walked over and untied her from the saddle.

She sat still, trying to regain herself as he undid the rawhide bindings which cruelly cut into her delicate hands. Hoffmann put his arms up to lift her down, she resisted and he pulled her down from the horse, standing her roughly on her feet.

She slapped his face hard. 'Bastard!'

Hoffmann raised the back of his hand and a fraction before striking, stopped. He took hold of her slight shoulder with a firm, powerful grip, like a father holding a child's doll. 'Don't yuh ever do that again.' His words were cold and hard, dark eyes burned controlled fury at her. The silence between them was almost physical, as she stared back angrily and then looked away. 'Yuh gonna do exactly as yuh told from now on, lady – if yuh don't want to get yuhself killed! 'Cos I've just about had mah belly full o' spoilt, city women ta last me the rest o' mah days!' Hoffman turned to the piebald she had been riding and stroked its muzzle, gently. 'Suggest yuh think on that some.' Suddenly he looked up and then yelled at her. 'Get behind them rocks!'

She looked surprised and did not move. 'Now!'

Bethan turned and ran as Jack slapped the rump of the horse and it galloped into cover near her. The gunfighter moved very quickly for a big man. He had drawn the Colt and was just in the cover of a boulder when Sourdough appeared from the defile thirty yards away on his small sorrel gelding, with a donkey behind him loaded up with enough provisions for a couple of weeks. 'Whoa! Hold on there, pilgrim – it's old Sourdough here. Don't shoot now.' The old man sat still for a moment, looking at the two bodies lying sprawled in the dust and then he whistled. 'Looks a-like I wuz jest in time. Heard the shots from down yonder. Yuh got 'em all, partner, or d'ya want any help?'

Hoffmann stepped out from behind the rock. 'There was only two of them, ol' timer. Mighty glad to see yuh, though.'

Sourdough caught sight of Bethan and gave a whoop of pleasure. 'Good ta see yer, Miss Bethan.' He trotted the horse over to her. 'Say. Yer looks a bit white round the gills, did they harm yer?'

'No, no, I'm fine.' She forced a smile.

'Gal's a mite shaken from me shootin' the two varmints from the front an' back o' her.'

The old man looked at Hoffmann and nodded. ''Course she is. Nasty experience. You'll be all right now with the two on us lookin' out fer yuh, Miss Bethan. So don't yer go worryin' none.'

Hoffmann strode over to the burro. Among the many provisions tied to its back was a wooden crate with black stencilled lettering on the side, marked: Dynamite.

'I said a six-pack, Sourdough. Yuh've got enough there ta blow up the danged county.'

The old man grinned through the grizzled white beard. 'Better safe 'n sorry, pilgrim. Yer never knows what yer might come across! Got a lot o' ammo too and a real good supply o' vittles!'

Hoffmann gave a faint smile. 'OK. Reckon yuh done well enough. Let's get going.'

The two men carried the bodies over to the rocks, noting the position so they could be brought back for burial in the felon's field at Pine Ridge in due course, and the party set off. Jack Hoffmann led with Bethan behind him and Sourdough at the rear. In a few minutes they had left the oppressive confines of the canyon behind. The group looked out to where the valley ahead merged with the prairie and spread out to become part of the great Wyoming plain, fading into distant ghost images and grey cloud castles that were cloaking the snow-capped mountains around them.

It was nearly one and a half hours later when the group led the horses through the rear of the spinney, out of sight of Thomas's ranch house, and set up their equipment. As Hoffmann had promised, it gave a clear, uninterrupted gun sweep over to the distant buildings. Sourdough unloaded the various packages and sacks from the sagging donkey. He set up a simple forked gun-support near to the edge of the covering foliage, consisting of a U-shaped piece of metal joined to the end of an iron rod, which he pushed into the ground, ready to support the long barrel. The buffalo gun was old, but well maintained. He offered it to Hoffmann, who looked the piece over.

The gunfighter nodded approval. 'Nice weapon, oldtimer! Single shot, though. Rare. Thought yuh said it was a repeater?'

'No, sir. But I kin reload, aim an' fire within seven seconds.'

Hoffmann gave him a slow look. 'Yeah?'

'Yep!'

'What type of shells?'

'.54 calibre. I loads the cases myself. Eighty grains!'

'Eighty? You'll blow the danged thing ta pieces, Sourdough. How long yuh been doin' that for?'

'Years.' He took the gun back. 'Funny thing, that's jest what a commercial traveller from the factory once said.' He rubbed an oily rag over the barrel with loving care. 'She kin take it though.' He gave a whoop. 'An' soon those evil sonsobitches are gonna see jest what eighty-grainers kin do from five hundred yards!' The old man winked, flicked the tail of his 'coonskin hat over his shoulder and lay down, placing the barrel into the metal fork. 'Yessir!'

Hoffmann walked across to the wooden crate, broke it open and took out two six-pack dynamite bundles complete with fuses and clipped them to each side of his gunbelt. He looked at Bethan and Sourdough, as the old man turned and sat on his haunches.

'Gonna try ta blow out the back o' the house an' drive them gunslicks out o' the front, so you kin use that ol' gun on them. An' that's not as crazy an idea as it sounds. The whole gang will be stunned like a nest o' sleepin' rattlers, 'cos there will have been one hell of a bang from this here six-pack o' dynamite. Once they've come to their senses, they'll just want to get outside, pronto, an' sneak around to the back, or just hide out a spell in them barns. There's nothin' but clear, open country viewed from the front o' the ranch house, an' once outside, they'll probably figure themselves pretty safe. Commotion an' noise will be comin' from the back of the house still, me shootin' away there like crazy an' all.

'There are three entrances to that place. Front, rear and one side door. They'll not come out of the back, 'cos it won't be there any more – just me pumping lead in every which way! That leaves the front an' side doors.' He pointed. 'Yuh kin see them clearly from here.' He nodded at Sourdough. 'Soon as yuh hear the explosion, be ready. Yuh first shot will give the game away of our intent, so yuh gonna have to be quick an' accurate at reloadin' an' firing again, before they can get back inside or duck into cover in a barn at the side!

'When I've cleaned everything up inside, I'll tie a 'kerchief to the end o' the Winchester and signal from the far side o' the ranch house. Yuh can both come down then. But be careful.

'Final point. Remember Sourdough, yuh first priority has got to be takin' out as many gunslicks as yuh can, cleanly. It's a long way off an' I knows yuh gonna do yuh best – but remember – don't send any lead into the house ifn yuh can avoid it. I'll have enough to think about without slugs a-comin' in through the windows!'

Sourdough nodded. 'Yes, sir. Do mah

darndest. But when she's fired up, this ol' buffalo gun is a pretty strong brute – somethin' may come in through the woodwork – even pine logs like those may not stop it!'

Hoffmann acknowledged. 'That's the risk I'm a-gonna take.'

The oldtimer lay down again, setting up the tall rear gun sight for distance. 'Yer can rely on old Sourdough to do his best.' He turned back. 'Ifn I does shoot yuh, Jack, it'll be accidental! Yuh won't hold no grudge will yuh?'

Hoffmann gave a rare smile. 'Not if I'm dead, oldtimer.'

Sourdough looked concerned and then turned back to his gun in rare silence. He was squinting down the long barrel when Hoffmann touched the brim of his stetson towards Bethan and swung up into the saddle.

'Don't worry none about yuh brother, Miss Bethan. He's locked up snug in a cabin about sixty yards out back of the ranch house. I'll be about half an hour, taking the route hidden by that gulch and work my way around the back.' He pointed, then headed Jess back through the trees. Hoffmann did not know if Daniel was in the cabin for certain, but thought the remark would ease her mind. He had noticed the small outbuilding when over at the ranch and had thought it the only practical place a person could be safely held against their will. He did not see Bethan's tear-filled eyes following his every movement, as horse and rider slowly vanished from sight.

The gunfighter took his time on the circuitous route, taking in every outbuilding, cow shed, barn and detailed part of the habitation that he could. No sign of life was to be seen and he knew that all the range-hands were now gone – paid off and looking for work elsewhere. Hoffman worked his way over to the small log cabin set among some tall conifer trees. He tied the reins to a branch and ran to the back wall.

'Can yuh hear me in there?'

An alert voice came back instantly. 'Sure! Who's that?'

'Name's Hoffmann. Gonna get yuh out o' there soon. You Daniel Mackenzie?'

'That's right.'

'Lay yuhself down on the floor, son, 'cos I'm a gonna blow out the back o' this ranch house!' The gunfighter moved carefully away from the rear of the cabin before its surprised occupant could reply and checked to see if all was clear, before sprinting over to the log pine constructed building. The back door opened easily to his hand and Hoffmann lit the fuse, rolling the dynamite bundle inside in a matter of seconds. He had time to sprint back to the cabin's cover and position himself with the Winchester before the horrendous explosion took place. Splintered wood, metal and glass flew in every direction in an enormous cloud of devastation, the sound of it an ear-shattering assault on the senses that Jack Hoffmann had been fully prepared for, but the men inside the ranch house were not.

The bounty hunter ran the distance into the ruin, assayed a barrage of shot from the hip-held Winchester as he entered what remained of a large kitchen. Whoever Thomas and Smith had employed, they were effective, recovering their sensibilities quickly, for immediately shots from a hand-gun and rifle were returned closely in his direction. As further shots rang back and forth, each man trying to gauge his enemy, Hoffmann heard Silas Smith's unmistakable voice shouting: 'Get out the front door and work round to cut the bastards off!' Jack was pleased to hear reference to himself as one of many, and wondered on the number of men Smith thought there were making the assault on his stronghold. He then heard a powerful, gruff voice bellow: 'Malachi, Nathan – get outa that goddamn door now, yuh yellow-bellied crittas!'

Hoffmann glimpsed two men running out of the doorway. Their fast exit was followed by two gun shots in his direction from someone still in the room, the shots covered rapid movements of another person, a huge man dressed in buckskins, rushing across the hallway and following the other two outside. As the front door shut behind them, a distant rifle shot rent the air; it was so powerful that Hoffmann distinctly heard window panes rattle in the house.

'Jesu! What the hell wuz that?'

Hoffmann was counting as the frightened words cut into his ear. 'One, two, three, four, five, six, se…' The report sounded for a second time, it echoed outside, rattling the windows once more. The gunfighter paced time again. 'Four, five, six, seven!' The far off sound of a third discharge from a large calibre rifle arrived again. Instantly blood, mucus and splintered bone exploded through a tall casement window, together with the body of the huge buckskin-clad gunman, most of his head blown away, splattering grey brain matter and body fluids across the oaken hallway.

Total silence reigned for long seconds. Hoffman took the opportunity to move silently into the hallway and position himself into a small box room that was empty. Through the gloom of smoke and carnage, he suddenly recognised the entrance to the sitting-room where he had sat with Thomas the day before. The gunfighter listened intently. He could hear a window squeaking slowly open and then Bill Thomas's voice.

'Nathan, Malachi – yer OK?'

Then another voice, cold and scared. 'They're dead, Mister Thomas – look over there! I'm making a run for it!'

Jack heard a door open and the voices of Smith and Thomas shouting obscene protests. Then a muffled sound of an outside door being slammed. Three seconds later, the bark of Sourdough's big buffalo gun rattled the house for one, final time and then as a grim silence returned, Jack Hoffmann suddenly rolled himself across the open doorway of the sitting-room. In an instant, his Peacemaker was cocked in one hand and the scattergun swung out of its holster in the other.

Sourdough stood beside Bethan and looked down to the ranch through a pair of field glasses. The smoking buffalo gun lay on the ground beside him, its long barrel still resting on the support rod, set into the earth. 'They're all dead Miss Bethan, all dead.' He lowered the glasses and turned to look at her. 'I sure do hate to be killin' again, all these years after the war's bin done an' over with. But I had ta do it. Wuz the only way to stop those evil varmints fer good and to help save yourn brother. Yer understands don't yer? I couldn't let Jack down!'

Bethan smiled and nodded slowly. Tears were still in her eyes. 'Yes I do. I'm most grateful for what you and Mister Hoffmann have done for Daniel and I. Perhaps one day you and Jack could visit us all in Washington?'

Sourdough's bright blue eyes twinkled pleasurably, like crusty diamonds. 'Well that's mighty good o' yer, Miss Bethan. I'm sure mah ol' buddy Jack an' me would be rightly honoured.' He turned towards the open plain. 'There's the signal, ma'am!' The old man lifted the field glasses and nodded. 'Yep! Let's git down there, pronto.'

The publishers hope that this book has given you enjoyable reading. Large Print Books are especially designed to be as easy to see and hold as possible. If you wish a complete list of our books please ask at your local library or write directly to:

Dales Large Print Books
Magna House, Long Preston,
Skipton, North Yorkshire.
BD23 4ND

This Large Print Book, for people
who cannot read normal print,
is published under the auspices of

THE ULVERSCROFT FOUNDATION

... we hope you have enjoyed this book.
Please think for a moment about those
who have worse eyesight than you ...
and are unable to even read or enjoy
Large Print without great difficulty.

You can help them by sending a
donation, large or small, to:

**The Ulverscroft Foundation,
1, The Green, Bradgate Road,
Anstey, Leicestershire, LE7 7FU,
England.**
or request a copy of our brochure for
more details.

The Foundation will use all donations
to assist those people who are visually
impaired and need special attention
with medical research, diagnosis
and treatment.

Thank you very much for your help.